PRAISE FOR
DIANE MARQUETTE

In Over My Head

"Diane Marquette knows the Chesapeake area like nobody else, and gives you the flavor of her unique environment in her new thriller, *In Over My Head*. This is a murder mystery with heart, and after reading it you'll add Jill McCormick to your list of favorite sleuths. Her next case can't come soon enough for me."
— Austin S. Camacho, author of the Hannibal Jones Detective Series

"For security guard Jill McCormick, nights are quiet on the graveyard shift at Chesapeake Conference Center, an upscale waterfront retreat for the nation's CEOs and politicos, until Dr. Roger Henderson checks in, then checks out—permanently. Drawing on her experience as a journalist and inspired by a true story, Marquette gleefully cultivates Maryland's Eastern Shore characters and scenery to pen a debut mystery as down-home and appealing as Maryland crab cakes, oyster fritters and sweet lemon tea."
— Marcia Talley, Agatha and Anthony award-winning author of *Through the Darkness*

"Diane Marquette's *In Over My Head* introduces you to her very personal writing style, wit, and her main character's spunky attitude in this fast-paced mystery."
— K. S. Brooks, award-winning author of *Lust for Danger*

"The heroine works as a security guard for the 'Chesapeake Conference Center,' but Jill longs to be hired as a deputy sheriff. Her lover (Mitch), who is a real deputy sheriff, disapproves of her ambition because he thinks the job is 'too dangerous for a woman.' On top of that edgy relationship, the dead body of an eminent physician from Philadelphia is discovered in the Center's swimming pool. Marquette's writing has been published in newspapers and magazines. Her prose is professional."

—John Goodspeed, Book Critic, the *Star Democrat*

Almost Mine

"A NOVELIST TO WATCH. Marquette demonstrates a very good ear for dialogue and professional writing skills. Her gifts shine with unmistakable talent."

—Anne Stinson, *The Star Democrat*

"A BOOK THAT SATISFIES THE SOUL *Almost Mine* is a tender story of unexpected love. First time novelist Diane Marquette's depiction of stepfamily dynamics is spot on. I loved the heroine's Gratitude Journal which was simultaneously comic and poignant. A compelling read."

—Annie Rogers, award-winning author of *A Dream Across Time* and *A Circle of Dreams*

"FOLLOW NEWLYWED HELEN as she falls in love with not only Adam, but also with his first grandchild, and lives with the threat baby Joey will be removed from her home by his unwed mother. Marquette's handling of a modern dilemma shines!"

—Terry L. White, author of *The Picker, Ancient Memories,* and *Mystick Moon*

IN OVER MY HEAD

by Diane Marquette

Cambridge Books

an imprint of

WriteWords, Inc.

CAMBRIDGE, MD 21613

ebooksonthe.net is a subsidiary of:

Write Words, Inc.
2934 Old Route 50
Cambridge, MD 21613

ISBN 1-59431-468-3 or 978-1-59431-468-1

Fax: 410-221-7510

Bowker Standard Address Number: 254-0304

Dedication

To my husband, who provides the love and encouragement for me to be a writer.

To my mother, who shared her love of books with me and who now works in the Library of Heaven.

Prologue

The cold chlorinated water revived the doctor. He instinctively gasped, inhaling water, not air. The pressure on the top of his head was released and he felt himself rising. When he broke the surface, he gasped again. This time he filled his lungs with damp air.

His head was still pounding from the blow he'd sustained. The figure leaning over him was silhouetted against the security light mounted on the roof. The doctor's eyes couldn't bring the face above him into focus.

His lungs burned and his heart hammered in his ears. Suddenly he felt pressure again on the top of his head, and just before he was forced down for the final time, he heard his wife's voice saying, "Hurry! Someone's coming!"

CHAPTER ONE

Tuesday's glorious sunrise made me think it was going to be a good day. There was no way then I could have known that by the end of the day I would have been questioned by the police, had a fight with my friend, and ticked off my boss. I don't even know if there was a beautiful sunset that evening. By then, I really didn't care.

For the most part, I like my job. I don't mind the commute or even the fact that I work the graveyard shift. I'm friendly with some of the people who work there; well, okay, just Sandy. Most of us agree that our boss can be a first class jerk, but I try not to let him get to me.

The Chesapeake Conference Center, where I work, is on 200 wooded acres along the eastern shore of Maryland's Chesapeake Bay. In the fall, winter, and spring months, the buildings of the United States Naval Academy in Annapolis can be seen from the conference center's west deck. The haze and humidity that hang in the air throughout the summer months give only a blurry view of the Bay through a sticky white mist.

We are less than an hour's drive from Washington, D.C., and regularly host meetings for many high-level government agencies, as well as businesses and corporations from all over the world. Occasionally we even get a visit from the President or other world leaders. What I like best about my job is its diversity. I work as a security guard on the campus, and every day is different, which helps me stay sane. In any given week, we may host a conference whose attendees are discussing national security issues, world peace, or international finance.

Tuesday's sunrise was finding me in a particularly sour mood, but I was hoping to blow off steam to Sandy when she came in at seven. Sandy's a Conference Assistant and says she loves her job. But I have trouble believing it when I see how awful Ted is to her.

I knew Sandy would probably have a lot to do for the group before their meeting, but hoped she'd give me a little time to vent.

The group was made up of fifty prominent doctors from all over the world. They'd been coming to the conference center for the past few years. Their coordinator has always been a Dr. Roger Henderson, a cardiologist from

Philadelphia and, based on what Sandy had said, more than a little bit neurotic. She said that he was very particular about all the arrangements for his meetings and could be pretty demanding. The group had arrived the day before and was supposed to have a welcome cocktail party and a poolside barbecue that evening. They were all in bed by the time I came in to work at midnight.

The job of everyone who works here is to make the guests happy. It's that simple. And if an employee can't find a way to do that, help is usually just a phone call away. With a support staff of over sixty people working around the clock seven days a week, there's always someone available who can respond. The confidence level runs high that we can control everything but the weather.

That's why we're one of the highest rated conference facilities in the eastern United States. And that's why I work there. I figure it will look great on my resume.

I walked along the gravel path to the conference building, a rustic structure with wooden shingles that have weathered to a smoky gray. I could see the white haze already hanging over the Bay that was off to my right about a hundred feet. I detoured to the parking lot to see if Sandy was there yet. She was just getting out of her car. "I need some therapy," I said in greeting.

"Good morning to you, too," she said. "How come you and your truck are still here? You haven't hurt anyone, I trust?" she asked, curiously eyeing the clipboard I was carrying.

"Not yet," I answered, as we headed for the building.

It was warm and humid for May, and the air conditioning that greeted us when we let ourselves in through the service entrance door felt refreshing. The draperies were drawn and only a few lights were lit in the main lobby, making the computer screen that Alan was watching seem unusually bright in the semidarkness. "Hey," he said without looking up. "Is it seven already?"

He closed the program he had been working in, rolled his chair back, and swiveled to face us, stretching and yawning. "Oh; hello, Jill," he said when he finally noticed me.

"Beautiful sunrise out there, Alan," Sandy said. "You might still be able to see it if you hurry. Anything I need to know for today?" She went into the adjacent kitchen to put her purse in her locker, and then walked around the lobby area, turning off lights, and opening drapes.

"Not really," he said, stifling another yawn. "According to the Food and Beverage Department's head count, they served fifty dinners last night, so all the doctors must have made their flights, and gotten themselves here on time. Looks like about half of them drove here. The rest took cabs or the airport shuttle. Dr. Henderson came in after dinner last night to say hello and have a quick look at the setup in the conference room. He requested a few last-minute changes — hey, big surprise, huh? But I've already taken care of them. All you have to do when they arrive at nine o'clock is smile. I know you can handle anything else that might come up; you always do, Sandy."

"Thanks. I appreciate your confidence. I'm sure everything will be fine. Their breakfast is at what time?" she asked, scanning some pages in a notebook.

"Eight," Alan answered. "But you know you may get a few showing up here early. Other than that, there's nothing else to tell you. I guess I'm outta here," he said, now standing and stretching with his arms overhead. "See you tomorrow, Sandy. Have a good one. How come you're here so late, Jill?"

"You don't really want to know, do you, Alan?" I asked.

"Probably not," he said.

I went to the front door to turn off the outside lights and looked down the long gravel path toward the dining building. The low gray dwelling was completely illuminated in the early morning haze, giving an impression of busyness inside. One wall was lined with tall windows, which spilled yellowish light onto the newly trimmed grass below. Those wonderful folks in the Food and Beverage Department had been hard at work for hours preparing breakfast for the guests.

I turned toward the third building in the vast triangle of lawn. I could see that there were several lights glowing from the windows of the second and third floors of the guest room building. There were a few early risers walking down the path that connected the guest quarters and the dining building. Tuesday was off and running.

Walking back to the front desk, I plopped into one of the chairs. I tossed the clipboard I'd been carrying onto the desk and massaged my temples. "This has been the longest damn night," I said. "And it was all our wonderful boss's idea."

"How so?" Sandy asked.

"Well, yesterday Ted asked me to do a 'special assignment' for him. He wanted me to go over some new security checklists he'd made up. He said I could come in later last night, and that it should only take a couple of hours, and then I could leave. Yeah, right. I got here a little after midnight and I'm just finishing up now. I've never seen so much paperwork in my life. It kept me sitting behind a desk most of the night. This 'special assignment' was a lot harder than jiggling doorknobs and chasing raccoons away from the Dumpster, which is what I usually end up doing most nights. I don't know what this checklist is all about—Ted didn't really say. Have you heard anything about the corporate office having a problem with the security here?"

"No, nothing," she said. "You know I would tell you if I had. Want some coffee?" I followed her into the kitchen off the front desk area. We leaned on the counter, each taking a tentative sip of coffee that Alan had made probably eight hours earlier. "I'm going to make some fresh coffee. This stuff's horrible," Sandy said. We dumped the contents of our mugs into the sink, and I watched Sandy empty and rinse the coffee pot.

"Thanks, but I'll get some at home," I said. "I need some sleep. Call you later." Before I could reach the door, my pager went off. "Aw, jeez, I was almost out of here." I squinted at the number being displayed. "It's the kitchen. Now what's their problem? Toaster jammed again? Maybe I should just ignore it."

"You know better than that," Sandy scolded. "If it's Maureen calling, you can be sure she knows you're still here. Don't take a chance. It would get back to Ted in a heartbeat."

I grabbed the receiver from the wall phone and punched in the three-digit extension for the main kitchen. "This better be good," I said when Maureen answered. Her words came fast, and I couldn't believe what I was hearing. "Say that again," I said, my eyes opening wide. "Be right there," I barked and bolted from the room without saying anything to Sandy.

I pushed through the front doors and sprinted down the path toward the dining building. Maureen was waiting for me on the back porch that led to the kitchen entrance.

She was pointing to the fenced area surrounding the nearby pool. "Over there, Jill," was all she said. I turned in the direction of the pool, picking up my pace.

When I cleared the open gate, I could see some people in the pool. It was hard to determine how many, but it was obvious there was indeed something wrong. I tossed my pager and watch onto one of the lounge chairs, and waded down the steps at the shallow end to meet them. Kitchen staffers Ricky and Warren were steering a man's floating body toward me. He was on his back, dead eyes staring at the heavens. I grabbed one of his outstretched arms and helped navigate him toward the edge of the pool. We awkwardly carried him up the steps, struggling to maintain our grip on his wet skin. We set him down as gently as we could on the rough concrete surface. I looked up to see several people standing just inside the gate.

"Has anyone called 911?" I asked, breathing hard.

"I did. Right after I paged you," I heard Maureen's voice say from somewhere in the crowd. "It's Dr. Henderson, isn't it?"

I didn't know. I'd never met the man. I looked at Ricky and Warren, who were both nodding yes.

CHAPTER TWO

The crowd parted for Maureen, who carried a pile of gold blankets. She handed one to Warren and another to Ricky. Then she handed me two. I suppose she felt it was more fitting for the security guard to cover the body. The other guys only worked in the kitchen. I gently placed the heavy blanket over the pale body, noticing how the surrounding oval of cement had become soaked.

The sound of distant sirens caused all heads to turn. I buckled my watch onto my wrist, hooked my pager onto the wet waistband of my pants, and draped my blanket around my shoulders.

I looked up to see Ted walking down the gravel path. Not rushing, just walking at his normal clip, adjusting his tie. He stepped up to join the crowd, who were now well inside the gate.

"I just got here," he said, smoothing his hair. "Jill, did you call Lyndon?" he asked, referring to the sheriff.

"No. Maureen called 911 just after she paged

me," I said. "I don't know who's responding."

The sound of tires on gravel caused all heads to turn again. The siren was abruptly cut off in mid-wail. We watched the ambulance pull up just on the other side of the fence, both its front doors flung open just as the vehicle came to a full stop. Only a few seconds behind, a car from the Bridgewood Sheriff's Department pulled up in a cloud of dust, its antenna whipping back and forth.

I squinted to see the face of the uniformed officer who was getting out of the squad car. Oh, no. God, please don't let it be.... Damn!

"Jill, why wasn't Lyndon called? Why is Mitch responding?" Ted demanded as he approached me. His fists were clenched, and he stopped just short of actually touching me, since he didn't want me dripping chlorinated water on his expensive Italian loafers.

Before I had a chance to straighten Ted out, Deputy Mitchell Garrett parted the crowd.

"What have you got here, Jill?" he asked, his warm brown eyes fixed on mine. My peripheral vision told me that the paramedics were kneeling on the concrete, lifting the blanket to look at the body.

"Well, Mitch," I said, careful not to let any emotion toward him show in my voice. "It's apparently Dr. Henderson, one of the guests.

Looks like he was taking an early morning swim. I was down at the conference building about twenty minutes ago when I got a page from Maureen. I hurried down here, and Ricky and Warren were in the pool trying to get Dr. Henderson out." I gestured again toward the body, as if there were any doubt who I was talking about. I noticed that the oval of moisture had gotten even bigger. "I helped them get him out of the water."

"Can you tell me what happened?" the deputy asked, flipping his notebook open. "You first, Ricky."

Not able to take his eyes off the shrouded body, Ricky told his audience how he had been carrying trays from the kitchen to the dining room to set up the breakfast buffet. A few guests had come in a bit early, begging for coffee, and Warren was just bringing out a pot when another guest hurried into the dining room, saying that someone was lying at the bottom of the pool. He and Warren rushed out to the pool and went in after the guy. He said he remembered thinking that he hoped someone was paging Security.

"And what time did all this happen, Ricky?" Mitch asked while writing, not looking up from his notebook.

Ricky looked at Warren, who answered the

question. "I guess it was close to 7:30. We weren't expecting anybody for breakfast until eight, so we were still setting everything up. I hadn't even brought out the coffee until those guys showed up asking for some."

"Ted, do you know this Dr. Henderson?" Mitch asked.

"Of course," he answered. "I mean most everybody here does. He's the coordinator for the group that's scheduled to meet here all week. He's from Philadelphia—a very prominent cardiologist. He's been coming here for a few years. I don't know what else I can tell you about him."

"Is his wife here?" Mitch asked.

"No, of course not," Ted answered. "Spouses don't attend these types of meetings. These aren't meant to be social affairs."

"I see," said Mitch, still writing. "I'll need to talk to someone else from his group. Find out how to contact the wife, and so on. Do you know who would be the best one to talk to about that?"

"Sandy would have all that information. She's down at the conference building, at the front desk." Ted said. "Why didn't Lyndon respond to this, Mitch?"

"Sheriff Clark was looking into a call he got on his way in to the office this morning. A domestic dispute. I'm going to contact him now. And I'll call the coroner's office," Mitch said. "So you guys may as well go," he said to the paramedics. "They'll take care of the body. Everybody else just stay here for a minute, will you?" Without waiting for anyone to answer, Mitch grabbed the two-way radio from his belt and started walking toward his car.

I very much wanted to go home, stand in a hot shower for ten minutes, and fall into my bed, but he hadn't said that we could go. We all stood there, awkwardly avoiding looking at each other or at the body.

When Mitch returned with his camera, he took about a dozen photos of the scene. He removed the soaked blanket and photographed the body, which was clad only in black swim trunks. He also snapped pictures of the area around the pool, including the path, fence, and gate, and took a few shots of all of us standing around looking like idiots. He wrote down the names of all the people standing poolside, before saying, "You can all go now. I know where to find you if I have any more questions."

"I want to say something to everyone first," Ted said quickly, causing everyone to stop. "I'd appreciate it if none of you talked to anyone else about this. Let's just keep this as quiet as possible. I mean, it's going to get out sooner or later, but I'd rather no one heard it from any of us, understood?" We all mumbled something appropriate and dispersed.

Still clutching my blanket around my shoulders, I was heading down the path toward the conference building, my truck, and home, when I heard Mitch's voice behind me. "Wait up, Jill." I slowed my pace. A little. "Are you okay? Did you really jump in to save that guy?" he asked.

"Yes, I'm okay," I said, not looking directly at him. "And no, I didn't jump in to save that guy. Anybody could see he was already dead. I was just helping Ricky and Warren."

"Still, what you did was pretty impressive," Mitch said.

"Impressive enough to get me another interview with the Sheriff's Department?" I asked, now turning to face him.

He started to reach his arms toward me, looked in both directions, and stopped, dropping them to his sides. "Jill, we've been through this a dozen times. You know I don't think being a deputy is a safe job for a woman."

"Why is it any safer for a man?" I asked. "Do you boys get the better bullets? Just because I don't carry a gun on the job here, doesn't mean I don't own one and know how to use it, too. Come on, admit it, you would feel threatened if you saw that I could do your job, and do it damn well, too, I might add."

"Look, I don't have time to talk about this now. Here's the coroner." We watched the black van back up the short access road to the pool. "Can I call you later?" Mitch asked.

"No. I'll either be in the shower or sleeping," I said as I turned away.

He called out after me, "Tell Sandy I'll be down in a little while to get some information from her, okay?" I turned to watch him jog away in the direction of the pool, his right hand keeping his gun from slapping against his thigh. That gun with those better bullets.

Sandy was standing in the doorway, and greeted me with a big hug. Even if she'd worn Italian loafers, she'd let me drip on them. "Are you okay?"

"Why does everyone keep asking me that?" I said loudly. "Don't I look okay?"

"No, as a matter of fact you don't," Sandy said, handing me a cup of steaming coffee. I caught sight of myself in the large mirror hanging in the lobby. She was right.

"Alice said the body in the pool was Dr. Henderson. Is that true? I just can't believe it! I was expecting him to come walking in here any minute to check on the conference room before his meeting, and then Alice tells me he's dead."

"Yeah, it's Henderson. Word sure got out fast. Alice must have been hiding in the bushes. I don't remember seeing her down there. I guess the doc was going for a swim before breakfast. We'll know more when the coroner gets through with him."

"Oh, Jill, please don't say that. I don't even want to think about that. What did Ted say?" Sandy asked.

"Not much. Look, I gotta get out of here. I'll call you later." I dropped the soaked blanket onto the mat at the front door. "Tell Alice she can have her blanket back. I don't need Housekeeping accusing me of stealing their property."

"Jill, I saw Mitch out there. Do you want to talk about it?" Sandy asked, her face softening.

"Not now. I'm going home to shower and get some sleep. I'm turning off my phone, too, so tell Ted and Mitch, and anybody else who cares that I can't be reached. I'll call you tonight. Oh, and by the way, Mitch said to tell you he'd be stopping by later to see you. He needs some info on Henderson."

CHAPTER THREE

I finally crawled into bed about ten o'clock. I'd showered, closed the blinds, and unplugged the phone. I cranked the AC down to 60, and fought my cat, Gunther, for the pillow.

When I woke up, I didn't know what day it was. The clock radio showed it was 6:56, and for a minute I thought I'd slept until the next morning. I sat up and peeked out through the edge of the blinds and could see the sun a good bit above the western horizon. It was still Tuesday. I had to be back at work in three hours. Damn.

On the pillow beside me, Gunther opened one eye, trying to decide if it was worth getting out of bed. "I'll feed you in a few minutes," I promised. He slowly rose and performed several different versions of stretching, then collapsed onto the bed again, and watched me as I headed into the bathroom to take my third shower in twenty-four hours. I dressed in my uniform of tan shirt and brown slacks. I laced on my thick-soled boots, which were still a little damp from my morning dip in the pool.

I waited until eight o'clock to call Sandy at home.

I didn't want Keith to intercept the call, and knew that by now he'd be curled up with the TV, watching the Orioles. I was reaching for the phone to dial Sandy's number, when it rang.

"Well, good evening, Miss McCormick," Sandy said. "Did you get some rest?"

"Yeah, I feel a lot better," I answered. "You at home?"

"No, I'm over at Pam's. Eddie had to work late. It was pizza night. The kids love it."

"I know you love it, too," I said. I pictured Sandy and her younger sister, both attractive petite blondes. Next to them, I always felt too tall, too athletic, and too plain. "What did I miss at work?"

"Oh, a few interesting things. Around 9:30 Ted and Mitch went down to the dining room and talked to the group. Apparently all the doctors had discussed the possibility of canceling, but decided to go ahead with their meeting. So, everything is still on, but they're all shaken up, of course. Their new coordinator is Dr. Thorpe, who seems awfully nice. He and Dr. Henderson are on staff at the same hospital in Philadelphia.

"And then, sometime early this afternoon, a reporter showed up. I think you'd recognize him;

he's been here before. He's with the *Chesapeake Banner.* He'd heard the call on the scanner. He wanted to know who had died and who found the body, and all the details. I was trying to get rid of him when Ted came out of his office and practically threw the guy out the door. I haven't seen Ted that upset in a long time."

"Well, it's not surprising. This is big news in this little town. Bad publicity."

"Maybe," said Sandy, "but you know how busy we are. We've got all the business we can handle. We're booked solid through the next year, and we've got a waiting list on top of that. People wouldn't cancel their meetings over this, would they? I really don't think Ted has anything to worry about, do you?"

"Probably not," I said. "So, what's happening with the body? Is Mitch taking care of having it IDed and claimed?" I asked.

"Yes. After the coroner left with Dr. Henderson's body, Ted and Mitch placed a call to Dr. Henderson's wife, I mean his widow. Just after they talked to her, Ted told me to let Reservations know that Mrs. Henderson was arriving sometime on Wednesday and would be staying in the executive suite," Sandy said.

"Wow! She's going to stay there at the conference center? Where her husband just died? I don't think

I could do that. That would be just too weird," I said. "Why isn't she staying at the Driftwood Inn or the B&B?" I wondered aloud.

"I have no idea. No one said anything about that to me, and I'm just trying to stay out of it," Sandy said.

"You sound a little funny; are you all right?" I asked.

"I guess," Sandy said. "Ted was very upset with me this morning for talking to that reporter. He swore that he'd told me to keep quiet about the accident, but he honestly did no such thing. And of course, he didn't even seem to care that he had upset me so much. I guess I was still so emotional over poor Dr. Henderson."

"Ted's such a jerk," I said. "I don't know why you just don't tell him where to go sometimes, Sandy. And so what if he fires you? It's not like you need to work, you know."

"I know," she said. "Keith reminded me of that again at dinner last night. I try not to even talk about work with Keith; you know it's never a safe topic with him. And I don't dare say a word to him about Dr. Henderson's death. He'll hear about it soon enough. Bridgewood is such a typical small town, and juicy news like that travels the fastest. Then I'll be in for another of Keith's tirades about his not wanting me to work."

"Whatever you say," I said, becoming bored with the conversation. "I guess I'll go in to work at ten o'clock as usual, since the group's still there. To tell you the truth, I wouldn't have minded if the group had cancelled. I could have used a few days off from that crazy place."

"Before you go in to work, maybe you should give Mitch a call. He's very worried about you," Sandy said.

"Well, that's tough," I answered. "I don't care if he is worried. He's happy with his job. He just doesn't want to see me get a job I might actually like."

"No, Jill, that's not it at all. Mitch said that you don't understand what happened with Sheriff Clark," Sandy said.

"And I suppose you do?" I asked. "Look, I don't care how many times Mitch tries to explain it; I still believe he sabotaged my interview. So, I just think it's best that we don't get back together. We're just not good for each other. I guess I have to choose between Mitch and my career." My chest was starting to tighten and I felt a headache coming on.

"Jill, you know you don't mean that. Mitch is such a wonderful guy. There's not a woman in Bridgewood, single or married, who wouldn't love to have a chance with him. And you can't deny the chemistry between you. Even I can feel it whenever I'm in the same room with you two.

"You have no idea how much he cares for you. I probably shouldn't tell you this, but he told me today that he couldn't get you out of his mind. He called you a distraction."

For some reason, this last comment really pushed me. "Oh, so now you're on his side, are you?" I said, raising my voice. "Well, that's just great. I suppose he asked you to put in a good word for him, is that it? Look, this really doesn't concern you, Sandy. I'm a big girl. I know what's best for me. I wish people would just quit telling me how to run my life. I'm sick of it!"

"Jill, please don't be upset with me. Maybe I shouldn't have gotten involved, but I care about you. You know that," Sandy said.

"If you care about me, then leave me the hell alone," I said, and slammed down the phone.

My hands were shaking and Gunther had scurried under the kitchen table. I walked to the refrigerator, opened the door, and then closed it. I went to the sink, filled a glass with water, and then set it down. I regretted that I'd talked to Sandy that way. I realized that she was not the one that I was mad at. I was still mad at Mitch. I considered calling her back, but knew that I needed more time to cool off. I'd apologize to her tomorrow. I always did.

I still had a little time before I needed to leave for work. I paced while I decided whether or not to call Mitch. He was the one that I should be venting to. I shouldn't let this good anger go to waste. I heard a car pull into my driveway, and parted the curtains enough to see that it was Mitch in his patrol car. I ran my fingers through my dark curly hair, still damp from the shower. "You can come out, Gunther. Mitch is here to save you," I said to the cat, who still sat hunched under the table. His large black body was in the shadows, and I could only see his white chin and paws, and his yellow eyes blinking out at me.

I let Mitch knock twice before I opened the door. His eyes showed a look of concern that used to comfort me, but tonight, I found it just annoying. I stepped back to let him in, but didn't say anything. He came in only far enough for me to get the door closed.

"I saw your lights on, and figured you were up. Are you doing better?" he asked tentatively. "You're not going in to work tonight, are you?"

"Of course," I said sharply. I tried to get my emotions in check. I wanted to say some things to him, but I didn't want to cry or yell or otherwise lose control while doing it. Maybe this wasn't the best time to do this after all. "I'm fine," I reassured us both. "Everything's fine."

Mitch took one step toward me. We were almost touching. His hands came up to rest on my shoulders, and he opened his mouth to speak. My pager on the kitchen table went off, and Mitch quickly jumped away from me. I realized that I had been holding my breath, and let it out quickly. I hurried to the pager to read the display. It showed Ted's office number at the conference center. I grabbed the cordless phone on the kitchen counter and punched in the number. He answered on the first ring.

It was a brief conversation. Ted told me that I needed to come in right away because Sheriff Clark wanted to talk to me about Henderson. The sheriff would be talking to other employees in the morning, but wanted to catch me tonight. I had no choice but to say that I was on my way.

"I've got to get to work," I announced to Mitch. "Your boss wants to talk to me."

"I know; that's one reason I came over. I don't think you should be going in to work tonight. You should make Sheriff Clark wait until tomorrow. I'm the one who needs to talk to you tonight, Jill," Mitch said, his dark eyes serious.

"Look, Mitch," I said firmly, then paused a beat and changed my tone. "All right, maybe we do need to talk about a few things. But I warn you. I'm still planning to be a deputy. You told me that

Peterson's thinking hard about retiring before the end of the year. I want his job. And I'm not going to let you ruin my chances this time. So, if there's anything other than my career that you want to talk to me about, I guess that would be okay."

I could see the look of relief spread over his face, and almost felt sorry for him. "Thanks, Jill," he said softly. We agreed to meet at the Copper Kettle in the morning, when I would be coming off my shift and he would be just about to start his.

CHAPTER FOUR

I started my truck and backed out quickly, leaving Mitch standing in my driveway beside his patrol car. He needed to know that I was still mad at him. I rolled both windows down and felt the sticky night air on my skin. I shook my head to clear away any more thoughts of Mitch, and tried to imagine what information Sheriff Clark thought I could give him. It would be interesting to see how Sheriff Clark treated me; I hadn't seen him since the doomed interview.

Ted had sounded anxious on the phone, and I didn't want to tick him off any more right now. He seemed more upset tonight than he had this morning when we'd found Dr. Henderson. Maybe he really was worried about business. I wondered if the accident would mean bad press for the conference center, but didn't really see how it could. We were booked solid for the next year, as Sandy had said. And there was a waiting list on top of that.

When I pulled onto the parking lot at 9:40, I saw the sheriff's car sitting at the fence near the pool, but didn't see the sheriff. I parked my truck next to the patrol car, got out, and stood listening for a minute. The patrol car's big engine purred gently and the powerful headlights pierced the darkness of the woods. The sounds of crickets and owls reached my ears, and the smell of pine needles hung heavy in the air. A short burst of static from the police radio broke through the litany of nature noises.

After a moment, I detected male voices coming from the direction of the pool. Ted must be chatting with the sheriff while they waited for me. I walked down the path, my boots crunching on the gravel.

I saw the two men standing inside the fenced pool area. They stood at the approximate spot where Dr. Henderson's body had been left by Ricky, Warren, and me after we'd pulled him out. There were several bright security lights mounted on the surrounding buildings. The chlorine smell was strong enough to override the pine needles. The bright blue water was illuminated from lights under its surface, and a few ripples gently lapped at the tiled edge.

"Evening, Miss McCormick," the sheriff said, tipping his hat.

"Jill, thanks for coming to talk to Sheriff Clark,"

Ted said. As if I'd really had a choice. "I take it you already know Lyndon?" he asked, nervously tapping a large flashlight against his right thigh.

"Miss McCormick here was interested in a job we had in my office a while back," the sheriff said, smiling slightly. "Too bad it was already taken by the time I got to talk to her about it. Too bad," he said, shaking his head slowly.

"What can I do for you, Sheriff? Ted said you wanted to see me," I said, eager to get this started and finished.

"Well, I'm talking to some of the folks who were here when this happened this morning. Quite a shock, I imagine. Now these are just some routine questions, you understand. Just following procedure. You were working here last night and this morning, is that right?"

"My normal shift is 10 p.m. to six in the morning. But last night was different. Ted had asked me to work on some paperwork concerning new security procedures. He told me that I could come in later and, since it would only take a couple of hours, I could go after that," I said.

"I see," Sheriff Clark said. "And so exactly what time were you here?"

"I got here about midnight, and didn't get finished the paperwork until almost seven. It took much longer than we thought it would. And then, of course, after the body was found, I guess I was here maybe another hour or so," I said. The sheriff wrote none of this down, which surprised me. I know how careful Mitch is to record every word that any witness ever tells him. He says his notes have saved him many times.

"Yes, Ted told me about those checklists he had you do. So, even though you were here at the time Dr. Henderson drowned, you weren't really doing your job? Your regular job, I mean?" he asked, his eyebrows raised.

"I was doing my job for that night," I said, my voice a bit louder. "I was working on the reports that my boss assigned me to do during that time. And since I haven't yet figured out how to be in two places at once, no, I wasn't really doing the job I would have normally been doing," I said.

"I see," he said, scratching his chin. "So where exactly did you do all this paperwork that had you so busy?"

"I sat in the main conference room for most of the time. But I did go to the bathroom twice. I thought that was okay to do," I said, glancing at Ted. He narrowed his eyes, showing me that he didn't appreciate my sarcasm.

"Okay, okay, I understand," said the sheriff. "But you weren't down in this area, near the pool, for any reason, the whole time you were here? That's what I'm trying to find out."

"No," I answered simply. Why the hell hadn't he just asked me that in the first place?

The sheriff turned away from me. "Well, Ted, looks like we've talked to everybody we can tonight. I'll be back in the morning to talk to the folks on the early shift. Miss McCormick," he said, tipping his hat.

I guess I was being dismissed. I looked at Ted, who was looking over his shoulder in the direction of the pool.

Feeling their eyes on me, I walked down the path toward the conference building. I felt annoyed with them, but couldn't really put my finger on why. Sheriff Clark had put me on the defensive. Was he suggesting that if I had been on my rounds, I might somehow have prevented Dr. Henderson's death? What would the chances have been that I would have been strolling by the pool at just the exact moment that morning when Dr. Henderson had gotten a cramp or whatever had happened to him, and could have saved him?

I yanked open the conference building's front door and felt a blast of cool, dry air. I saw Eve, the Conference Assistant who worked the middle shift between Sandy's and Alan's, on the phone. She smiled and waved, and I went into the kitchen to get a mug coffee. Eve came in a minute later and refilled her own mug.

"Has the sheriff talked to you?" she asked.

"Just now," I said, my jaw tight. "What is it about that guy?"

"I don't know," Eve said, smiling. "He's just a good old boy, I guess. Polite, but somehow condescending."

"Exactly," I replied.

"Well, I couldn't tell him a thing," Eve said. "I wasn't here for any of it. I thought he seemed almost relieved. It's almost as if he doesn't want anybody to tell him anything he has to write in his report. Just a simple accident. No big deal. Over and done."

"You're right," I said. "I got the same feeling."

"Hello, ladies," Alan said from the doorway. "Eve, I'm a little early. If you want to go ahead and leave, it's okay with me."

"Thanks, Alan. Oh, I'm supposed to tell you that Sheriff Clark wants to talk to you. He'll be back about six tomorrow morning to talk to the kitchen and housekeeping staff and said to tell you that he'd see you then. He knows you leave at seven o'clock," Eve said.

"I don't know what he thinks I can tell him. I don't know a thing," Alan said.

"Same here," Eve said.

"Jill, you'd be more likely to have seen something.

Has the sheriff talked to you yet?" Alan asked.

"He has, and no, I didn't see a thing. Remember I was tied up half the night and into the morning with that damned assignment from Ted. Maybe if I hadn't been doing that, the guy might not have drowned," I said.

"You can't really believe that, Jill," Eve said. "It was no one's fault. What happened to the doctor was an accident. There was nothing that anyone could have done unless they were right there with him. He went swimming alone early in the morning. Probably before anyone else was even up. He must have had some kind of medical condition. Maybe he had a heart attack or something. Did anyone think about that?" Eve asked. "That would be so strange, wouldn't it? I mean, he was a cardiologist, after all."

"Well, what's done is done," I said. "We can't change any of it. I need to get to work. Back to doing my real job," I said. "I'll check the conference room while I'm here."

I took my coffee with me and walked down the hall to the lobby. I left my mug on the desk, and approached a set of heavy wooden doors that led to the main conference room. When I turned the knobs, the doors silently swung open, and I walked into the dark room. I extended my right arm out until my fingers touched the wall. I punched all of the light switches, and the enormous room was instantly ablaze.

The forest green carpeting and dark paneled walls provided a plush background for the stark furniture in the room. A dozen rectangular oak tables had been set up in a U-shaped configuration. There were fifty notepads and fifty pens bearing the Chesapeake Conference Center logo perfectly lined up, one of each at each place. Fifty plush burgundy chairs were placed at regular intervals around the tables.

I heard someone behind me, and turned as Alan entered the room. "I need to double-check some of the AV equipment for tomorrow's meeting," he said. I watched him go to the front of the room, and turn on a slide projector, which cast an image of some type of surgical procedure being performed. He adjusted the focus and advanced the carousel to view the next slide.

I turned toward the bank of windows that faced the woods. The blackness of the glass cast my reflection back at me, and I checked each window to make sure that it was closed and locked. I made sure that the fire exit door was secure, too. "See you later, Alan," I called, as I left the room. I finished my coffee and put my mug in the kitchen.

CHAPTER FIVE

I left by the back door, which was at the end of a small supply room. Cases of notepads, copier paper, and other office supplies lined the walls on either side of the door. I took the large flashlight that was hanging by the door. Stepping out into the damp air again, I heard the crickets and owls. I let the door close behind me, checking to make sure it was locked. Since I had begun working as the night security guard, there had only been two incidents of vandalism, both minor and both done by high school kids. It was a large area for one person to cover, and some nights I probably walked close to five miles.

I headed along the gravel path toward the building that serves as the guests' quarters. I checked my watch. It was nearly 11:30, and there were only a few lighted windows on the second and third floors. As I walked toward the parking lot that serves the guest building, I heard a car approaching. I stopped at the edge of the road to see who was out at this late hour. A small dark sedan that had seen better days stopped where I stood. By the light from the dashboard, I identified the driver as the reporter Sandy had told me about.

"Good evening," he said, sliding the gear into park. "I heard about the drowning out here today. I was wondering if I could have a few minutes of your time?"

"Sorry. You'll need to come back in the morning and see Ted Savin. He's the General Manager," I said.

He cleared his throat. "Yes, I know. To tell you the truth," he said, "I was here this afternoon, and, well, I couldn't see him."

"Sorry, there's nothing I can do. I don't know anything," I said firmly.

"Oh, don't be so modest, Miss...?" He paused, waiting for me to fill in the blank. When I didn't, he stretched his head and neck through the open window, trying to read my nametag in the darkness. "Jill McCormick," he stated. He reached for a notepad on the seat beside him and wrote it down. "Come on, I'm sure you know everything that goes on around here. You're Security, aren't you?

"Yes," I answered.

"You have to be very capable to work here. This place gets a lot of VIPs in here all the time. I'm sure you've seen it all. How many years have you worked here?"

"Two," I answered.

"Hey, then, you must have been here for some of those really hush-hush meetings, huh? I know you folks like to keep things pretty quiet, but word gets out, you know what I mean? You must have been here during that big United Nations meeting, right? And, you would have been here for the Mideast Peace Talks a year or so ago, right? All those world leaders were here for that. Hey, did you get to meet the President and the Prime Minister and the head of the CIA, and all those people? Wow, that must have really been something."

"Yes," I said.

"I'll bet you need all kinds of special security clearance to work here for that, huh?"

"Yes," I said. If I kept giving him one-syllable answers, maybe he'd go away.

"So, what else can you tell me about what happened today?" he said.

"Nothing," I said.

"I see," he said. "Look, I'm kind of on a deadline here, and so anything you could tell me would really help me out."

"Sorry," I said.

"Well, thanks for nothing." He clenched his jaw, and as he gunned the engine and shifted into drive, I heard him cursing just under his breath.

I watched as he wildly swung the car in a U-turn and drove quickly down the road, a cloud of gray dust visible through the red of his taillights.

I doubted he'd be back again. He'd just have to write his article using the few details he already had.

Too bad. He wasn't going to get any information from me about the drowning or anything else. I watched the taillights until the car had gone down the road and around the bend. Instead of proceeding to the guest building, I changed direction and walked over toward the pool. I stood just inside the gate and thought about the body I had helped pull out just about fifteen hours earlier.

Although I had never met Dr. Henderson, I'd heard some of the employees talk about him. I tried to remember what they'd said. I knew there was a Mrs. Henderson, and that she was coming to the conference center. He had looked to be in his fifties. Did he have children? Grandchildren? Had his wife told them that he wouldn't be coming home?

I thought about what it would be like to drown. From everything I'd ever learned about drowning, it was a particularly agonizing way to die. For whatever reason, Dr. Henderson had not been able to save himself. Maybe he did have a heart attack—he was the right age for it. Maybe he had some kind of a seizure in the water. If only someone had been with him, another doctor, maybe they could have helped him.

I decided to check the kitchen doors and windows since I was so close. Next stop would be the guest quarters.

After that, I would take a break and give some thought to what I wanted to say to Mitch at breakfast.

Chapter Six

There was only one employee at the registration desk. It was Deirdre and she was reading a magazine. "Hey, how's it going, Jill?" she asked, looking up.

"Okay," I answered. "Anything new over here?"

"No. We're all pretty much still in shock about Dr. Henderson. What a shame, huh?"

"Yeah," I said. "Were you here when he checked in yesterday?"

"No, I was off yesterday. I'm not sure who was on duty then. Is it important?" she asked.

"No. Just curious," I said. "Sandy said that his wife is coming here sometime later today."

"That's right. Ted said we'd better all be very sensitive to her because of the situation," Deirdre said.

"That's a good one. Ted doesn't know the first thing about being sensitive."

"Well, he may have been referring to the incident when Mrs. Henderson stayed here about a year ago," she said.

"Oh?" I said. "What's that all about?"

"Mrs. Henderson is some sort of bank executive. Her husband recommended that her financial group have their annual meeting here. I don't remember many of the details, but there was apparently some problem with her room and she accused one of the housekeepers of something. I remember she got Ted involved, and I think the housekeeper was fired."

"I never knew anything about that," I said.

"Well, that may be the incident that Ted was referring to. I remember hearing at the time that Mrs. Henderson made things pretty uncomfortable for him," Deirdre said.

I had a hard time imagining a situation where I would feel sorry for Ted.

"Dr. Thorpe is going to be the new leader for the group while they're here. I have a message here from Sandy that he wants to be told when Mrs. Henderson arrives."

"I wonder what that's all about?" I asked.

"Probably just to convey the condolences of the group, I guess," she said.

"Well, I'm off for my rounds. Page me if you need me, okay?" I said, walking toward the back of the building.

"Sure will," Deirdre said.

I let myself out the back entrance, which led to the guest building parking lot. I scanned the Mercedes and Volvos that sat in the dimly lit lot. No one could mistake this for the employee parking area. I scanned the road for any sign of the reporter or his car, but found none.

I walked around to the opposite side of the building and checked to make sure the other exterior doors were locked.

I passed most of the night sitting on the porch of the dining facility. I had to spray myself with "Off" a few times because of the huge mosquito population that I seem to attract. Still it was a great place to do some serious thinking. I could hear the waves from the Bay on the other side of the building, and my pager didn't go off once. I began hearing cars come down the road around four o'clock— employees coming in for the early shift.

Part of me couldn't stop feeling angry with Mitch for screwing up my interview with the sheriff. There had been an opening in the department, and damn it, I was qualified for the job. I'd taken every course available that dealt with law enforcement. I'd put in some serious time here on the security detail. I'd also learned a lot from the different people that I had worked with in this job—the Secret Service, the FBI, and the state police. I had arranged an appointment for an interview with

Sheriff Clark for the deputy position. When I got there, he told me the job had already been filled. He said that Mitch had led him to believe that I really wasn't serious about taking the job, and so he had filled it.

Mitch had tried to explain. Many times. He maintained his innocence about telling the sheriff I didn't want the job. But he couldn't hide the fact that he was relieved that I hadn't gotten it.

Another part of me kept reinforcing that I had strong feelings for Mitch. We'd been seeing each other for almost six months. Sandy was right about the attraction between us. It was so strong it scared me. But why did we argue so much? I wondered if I wasn't the one doing the sabotaging to our relationship. Maybe I didn't really want a serious relationship with anyone. Maybe somewhere deep in my subconscious I didn't want to be that involved with anyone. Maybe I was afraid I'd be hurt by Mitch. Maybe I was afraid of hurting him. Sitting here thinking about Mitch made my heart heavy. I had to admit to myself that I really did care deeply for him. Was it love? And what was I going to do about it if it was?

If we were going to meet in a few hours for breakfast, I'd have to fight to keep focused on the discussion, and not get distracted by the feelings I had just acknowledged to myself. I used my small flashlight to check my watch. Almost five.

A voice in the near-darkness startled me. "Jill?"

"Who is it?" I asked, straining to see down the path.

"It's me, Alice," came the reply.

I shined the flashlight in her direction. Alice approached the porch, carrying a box of trash bags and a feather duster. She stood at the bottom of the steps, the small security light overhead shining down on her. She set down the box and duster. Her uniform was a size too small for her ample shape. She pulled at the shirt and pants, trying to stretch the fabric.

"Are you just getting here?" I asked.

"Yes, I came in early. Have you heard?" she asked, eyes wide behind her thick glasses. "The sheriff is going to interrogate all of us today! I wonder why he's going to do that? He must think something's fishy, don't you think?"

"Not really," I said. "I'm sure he's just following procedure."

"I don't know," Alice said, slowly shaking her head. "Ricky and Warren said that Dr. Henderson was stiff when they pulled him out of the pool. That means he'd been dead for a long time, doesn't it? Was he already stiff, Jill? You helped pull him out, didn't you?" she asked, becoming a little excited. "Just imagine, all those doctors here, and nobody could save him, because he was already dead."

"Look, Alice, it's not good for you to be spreading stories like this. It was an accident. It's the job of the Sheriff's Department to file a report. That's all there is to it," I said impatiently.

"Well, I'm just repeating what I heard. I wouldn't really know anything about this sort of thing," Alice said impatiently. "All is know is that his towels had been used the night before." She took off her glasses and polished them on her shirttail, which was hanging out of her pants.

I stared at her. "What's that got to do with anything?" I asked.

"Well, I could tell that he'd used his towels the night before, but they had dried, you see. They were all bunched up, of course. He'd used them all—both sets. But he didn't take a shower or a bath. The little bar of soap was still wrapped up," Alice said excitedly.

I still wasn't following her line of thinking. "Alice, I don't see what any of this has to do with anything," I said.

She smiled slightly, happy with the fact that she understood something that I obviously didn't. "People usually take baths at night," she said slowly. "But he couldn't have taken a bath that night because there was no ring around the tub.

In the morning, people almost always take showers. But he couldn't have taken a shower that morning because the towels were already dry when I came in to clean. I know these things. It's my job," she added, pushing her glasses back to the top of her nose.

I watched her as she stood staring at me. Then she added, "And besides, the little bar of soap was still wrapped up."

"You already said that," I replied. I really didn't want to continue this conversation, which was making me feel uneasy. I checked my watch, and stood up. "I need to go take care of some things, Alice."

I started down the steps and was surprised to see Sheriff Clark standing a few yards down the path. I hadn't heard him approach. How long had he been standing there? I hoped that he hadn't overheard the nonsense that Alice had been saying. And I hoped that if he had, he hadn't thought that I shared her bizarre thoughts.

"Morning, ladies," he said, as he tipped his hat. "Just thought I'd catch some of the early birds here as they come in to work. Just a few questions, you know."

"Well, since we've already talked, I'll leave you and Alice here," I said, taking off in the direction of the kitchen.

CHAPTER SEVEN

The parking lot of the Copper Kettle is always full. It's open twenty-four hours a day and the waitresses never let your coffee cup get empty. I squeezed my truck between a motorcycle and a camper at the far end of the side lot. I'd seen a patrol car parked near the front door, but didn't think it was Mitch's.

I was a little early. I wanted to relax a few minutes before I saw him. I studied the flat-roofed buildings of the restaurant. This place had been here as long as I could remember. The yellow stucco walls were stained and cracked, and vines were clinging to the walls, trying to escape the busy parking lot. I couldn't remember it ever being closed— not for holidays, or even when the owner's wife died. It was just business as usual that day, although I think they may have opened later, after the funeral.

There was a steady stream of patrons coming and going through the front door, which remained open, allowing some of the conditioned air to escape. I went inside, and was lucky enough to snag a booth near the door to the kitchen. I had a good view of the parking lot and a few minutes later saw Mitch's patrol car enter and drive around the side of the building.

I watched Mitch walk into the Copper Kettle; so did almost everyone else. His starched shirt, the color of coffee with cream, was tucked into brown fitted trousers. The heavy black leather belt, which held his gun, radio, and all the other gear necessary to do his job, hung low on his hips. He had left his brown cowboy-style hat in the car.

People turned in their seats to wish him a good morning. He smiled, shaking hands, patting people on the back, his eyes searching the room until he spotted me.

Before he could get to my booth, Penny blocked his way, a coffee pot in each hand. His six-foot frame towered over her. She must have said something cute because he gave her a wink and a grin and pointed over her head toward me. Penny turned, cracked her gum in my direction, and with a toss of her head, went back to her tables.

"Hi, I hope you just got here," he said, sliding onto the seat across from me.

"I see you almost had a date," I said, nodding toward the kitchen.

"Penny? Oh, come on, I'm just in here all the time," he said, a little color coming to his cheeks.

"She didn't look too happy when you told her you were here to meet me," I said.

"Come on, Jill, don't be like this," he said with a smile. "I thought we were going to talk about us. I don't have much time," Mitch said. He signaled for Rose, the older waitress.

Rose hurried up to the table, her gaze directed at Mitch. "Tell me what I can do for you today, Mitch. And I hope it doesn't have anything to do with this place," Rose said, winking at me. She reached for her pad, and we gave her our order. She put our order in, quickly returning with two mugs of scalding coffee.

"Jill, I've been going over and over everything that's happened between us lately, and I just don't see how this has gotten so out of hand. I know you don't want me to talk about the deputy job, so I won't. But, please, won't you tell me what I've done that is so wrong that you've shut me out of your life?"

I still couldn't get over how handsome he was, and not just because he was in uniform; although that had always held a certain charm for me. I knew in my heart that Mitch really did care for me. As usual, his dark eyes were seeing only me. He sat focused, ready to listen to what I was going to say.

"I'm not sure even I know what's happened between us," I said. "I don't know if the interview mess was really about you or about me. I just feel so frustrated about my job. The conference center is such a dead end for me, and I'm starting to feel desperate to make a change. Sure, I've had some great experiences there, but it's time to move on. I saw the deputy's job as a way out, but we both know how that went."

"As I've tried to explain to you," Mitch said, "I don't think that being a deputy is a safe job for a woman. It's not that I don't think that a woman can do the job.

"There's a difference. And besides, you don't know Sheriff Clark like I do. He's the one who has doubts that a woman can do the job. He's never hired a woman, except as a dispatcher. He's required by law to give everyone a fair chance, but all it took was for a man to have the first interview, and he gave him the job right away. That may not be the right thing to do, but that's what he did. There are other jobs around besides ones in law enforcement. You're smart and you've got a good education, Jill, you could do anything you want to do," Mitch said.

"You know my heart's set on law enforcement, Mitch," I said. "Maybe if I went to the other side of the Chesapeake Bay. They've got plenty of female police officers and female deputies in Annapolis and Baltimore and Washington. But I'm really not interested in moving or having such a long commute. I especially don't want to move," I repeated, as I made eye contact with him.

"Well, there's at least one thing we agree on," he said, as he slid his hand across the table to cover mine.

"You seem to have had this thing about law enforcement ever since I've known you. I've never really heard you talk about doing anything else."

"As I've told you, it's because of my dad, I guess. I don't remember too much before he was killed, but I remember how sad my mother was from then on. I don't think she ever got over it. Even though I was very young, I guess something just stuck with me that I needed to get the bad guy who shot my daddy, the nice policeman. Maybe I still feel that I have to get that bad guy, to make my mother happy again," I said, looking out the window.

"Jill, your Mom isn't aware of much anymore; she wouldn't even know if you became a deputy," Mitch said gently. "I still think you need to broaden your horizons. Is there someone you can talk to about other careers? I think you need to let go of this law enforcement fantasy," Mitch said, as Rose slid our plates in front of us.

He must have realized how his words sounded, and he looked up quickly, waiting for a reaction from me. I closed my eyes for a few seconds. "I know you didn't mean that the way it sounded, Mitch. But you may be right. I think I will talk to one of the counselors at the college."

I wasn't sure how sincere I was about what I heard myself saying, but it seemed a good way to end the conversation.

Mitch let out the breath that he had been holding. "That sounds like a plan. Keep me posted?"

"You'll be the first," I answered. "Well, I see we ending up talking about my career anyway, even though we agreed we wouldn't."

"I know," he said. "But I guess it's all connected, isn't it? I care so much for you, Jill, and I want you, and us, to be happy. So, we'll still be all right?" he asked, brown eyes warm and sincere.

I smiled and answered, "I guess so."

Mitch finished eating, checked his watch, and slid out of the booth. He gave my shoulder a little squeeze and said, "I'll stop by later?"

"Sure," I said, giving him a weak smile. He left a couple of bills under his mug, and took the check to the register. I watched him get in line to wait his turn to pay, and instantly Penny was on him again. She stood just off to his side, facing me as she animatedly talked to Mitch. She was standing so close to him that he had difficulty getting his wallet out. His back was to me, but I could see him repeatedly shaking his head in response to whatever line of crap she was giving him. Someone in the far booth called her name, and she reluctantly retreated from Mitch. While pocketing his change, he turned to see if I had been watching. He slowly shook his head, shrugged his shoulders, gave me his boyish grin, and walked out the door.

I took my time finishing my breakfast, Rose refilling my mug even before it needed it.

I considered what Mitch and I had discussed, and knew I had to give some serious thought about making a career change. The main source of my frustration at the conference center was all the politics. Even though a company based in New York owned it, the corporate office didn't really have much of a hand in the day-to-day running of the place. That they entrusted to our boy, Ted. They had no idea what a poor manager he was or that the only reason the place was so successful was that he had surrounded himself with talented and conscientious people. His employees were everything that he was not. On the rare occasion that someone from the corporate office did visit the conference center, Ted looked good, but only because of the people under him. I had a real problem working for someone that I didn't have a shred of respect for.

I knew when I took the job as security guard nearly two years ago that it wouldn't be a job I'd stay in forever. I was using it only as a stepping-stone to further my pursuit of a career in law enforcement. I didn't care for most of the people who worked there. I was grateful that I worked the overnight shift, so that I wouldn't have to deal with all the office people who were there during the day. Sandy was always telling me enough stuff about what went on during the day for me to know that I didn't want to be there. It wouldn't take much for me to tell one of them off big time, and it would probably be Ted. Even if I hated my job, I didn't need to get fired from it.

I'd have to call Sandy when I got home. I still owed her an apology. She'd be glad to hear that Mitch and I were back together, at least for the foreseeable future. She was the mother I couldn't talk to anymore.

CHAPTER EIGHT

The Bayview Nursing Center has no bay view, although none of the residents seems to notice. Most spend their days lying in bed or in wheelchairs dozing in gloomy hallways. The rest of them can't see past their windows anyway.

"Good morning, Mavis. How is she today?" I asked as I signed the ledger.

"Pretty good, Miss Jill. She had a real good night. She don't cause no problem, you know that. I heard about the trouble over at your place. A real shame it is. A nice young man like that drowning. A doctor, too. What a shame. Did he have family?"

"A wife. I don't know about children," I said. I really didn't feel like chit-chatting about the topic to one more person. I gave a little nod as I quickly headed down the hall.

A few of the more alert folks lining the hallway greeted me with smiles and waves. One woman reached out to touch my sleeve. "You're coming back, aren't you? Coming to take me home?"

"Not today, ma'am," I said, as I continued walking briskly toward the corner.

I nodded to the nurse at the desk who was on the phone, and stopped outside the closed door to Room 110. I slowly pushed it open with my knuckle and peered into the dim room. Mom was sitting in a wheelchair, her back to the door. She faced the large window, but the heavy curtains were closed. It didn't matter.

As I stood in the doorway looking at the familiar outline of her head and shoulders, it seemed almost possible that she'd hear me, turn, and say my name. It seemed almost possible that she might still be my mother as I remembered her. But as I watched her head droop and her shoulders slump, I knew there would never be any possibility of that happening. She was simply gone.

"Hi, Mom," I forced myself to say in a cheerful voice. "Mavis tells me you had a good night."

I stood between her and the window until I could be sure that she noticed me. She blinked and looked at my face, but there was no recognition. I turned the wheelchair so that it faced the only other chair in the room. I sat, studying her face. She seemed to be studying mine, too, but I knew there would never be any sign that she knew who I was. I took her hand in mine; it was limp and cool. The silence hung heavy in the dim room.

"Mom, I wanted to talk to you about a few things. Remember Mitch, the deputy I told you about? Oh, I know what you're going to say. You don't think I should date someone who's in law enforcement. I know you don't want me to go through what you went through when you lost Dad." I gently placed her hand back in her lap. I stood and walked a few feet away. When I turned, she still had the same expression on her face.

"Well, the thing is, we've had a fight, and I'm not really sure what it was about. Now it doesn't seem so important anyway. And besides that, I miss him. I really don't like being mad at him." She continued to look at me.

"He really cares about me, Mom. He loves me. But, I'm not sure we're really good for each other. We're both pretty headstrong. But I don't have to tell you that, do I? And Mitch is very dedicated to his job. I know I'm lucky to have him, but I don't know exactly why I can't seem to let my guard down around him. It's as if I have to prove myself all the time. That's what our big fight was about. Why do you think that is, Mom? Have I always been like that? You know me better than anyone else after 32 years." She was looking at the floor now.

"Well, I just thought you might have something to add," I said. I went to the window and opened the heavy brown print drapes to reveal the partly cloudy sky. "We're supposed to get a bad thunderstorm later. It's been so hot and humid, it would be a relief to get some rain. Remember how I used to be so afraid of thunderstorms? You'd always let me sleep with you, do you remember? We'll, I've pretty much outgrown them, so you don't have to worry about that anymore," I said.

"Sandy's doing fine. She tries so hard to keep Mitch and me together. She thinks we're good for each other, but I just don't know if I agree with her. Sandy's been babysitting Pam's kids sometimes. That has to be hard for her. It's taken such a long time for her to get over Emma. I can't imagine what it would feel like to lose a child. Maybe that's something no one can really get over. Maybe they just go around it. I know how much it hurts to lose a father. And a mother. But losing a child would have to be worst of all. We're not supposed to outlive our children. That's too cruel." Mom was looking at me again now, as though she might speak at any moment.

"Sandy and Keith are not doing well at all. He's no support to her. And they're always fighting about her working at the conference center. He just can't stand the fact that she wants to work. It's a sort of therapy for her, I think," I said, as I sat down again. "Sandy's such a caring person. She really does a great job. They're lucky to have her, although Ted has no appreciation for anyone except himself."

I went on to tell her about the drowning at the conference center, grateful she'd be the one person who wouldn't ask questions.

I looked at Mom's face. Could she understand my words? How could I ever know? She knew what it was like to lose her spouse and she hadn't had an easy time of it working and raising me, too. After Dad was killed, we moved from Baltimore to the Eastern Shore of Maryland because Mom believed it was a better environment to raise her daughter. She hated the city that her husband had loved. And he had died doing his job protecting that city.

I know Mom thought she was doing what was best for me, but it meant leaving my friends. After my father died, I'd become withdrawn and had a difficult time making new friends. It wasn't until junior high school that I'd met Pam and we'd remained friends ever since. But since working at the conference center, I'd become even closer to her big sister, Sandy.

I had met Mitch through Pam. He was a friend of Eddie's, Pam's husband. Since I refuse to go out on blind dates, Pam had to arrange an "accidental" meeting at her house one night. For three days after I met Mitch, I couldn't stop thinking about him. I was even considering calling him for a date when he called me instead. We've been together about six months, most of them good ones. Sandy was right — the chemistry was undeniable.

Mom was staring at the floor now. "Well, I'd better be getting home. I need to get some sleep," I said. The sound of my voice caused her to look at me. I stopped seeing that as an encouraging sign long ago. "I'll try to come back on Saturday, if not before," I said. I kissed the top of her head, and gave her hand a final squeeze. There was the tiniest of smiles on her lips as I closed the door.

CHAPTER NINE

Feeling that I needed to call Sandy before I could sleep, I dialed the number for the conference center front desk a little after ten. The first thing I did was apologize. No explanation. Just said I was sorry. Sandy forgave me even before I had the sentence out of my mouth. Then she said that the sheriff had just left.

"That guy is tireless," I said. "He must have talked to every employee twice by now."

"Some people are saying that the sheriff thinks something is not right about Dr. Henderson's death," Sandy said. "This whole incident has gotten everyone talking."

I gave Sandy a very abbreviated version of Alice's observations about Henderson's towels and tub. "Incidentally, Mitch didn't say anything about the investigation at breakfast," I said casually.

"Oh, so you two are back together now?" she asked timidly.

"I don't know, Sandy," I said. "At least we're not fighting at the moment. That's about all I can tell you for sure. It's hard having a relationship when we're always passing each other going to and from our shifts. Anyway, he's going to stop by my house later. Maybe he'll have some news about the autopsy."

"Oh, I can't bear to even think about that," Sandy said. "Poor Mrs. Henderson will be here today. I guess Ted will talk with her. And she'll probably have to go see about the arrangements for Dr. Henderson's body. That poor woman. Imagine sending your husband off on a business trip and then getting a call saying that he's drowned."

"Yeah, that would be pretty rough," I said. "I understand from Deirdre that Mrs. H. has been there before."

"That's right, but it's been a long time, probably more than a year ago," she said.

"When we found the body yesterday morning, Ted told Mitch that Mrs. H. never came here with her husband," I said.

"That's true. She came for a business meeting of her own. Something to do with investments, I think."

"That's what Deirdre remembered, too," I said. "She also said that there was a big stink about some problem with one of the housekeepers. Do you know anything about that?"

"As I recall, Mrs. Henderson had a complaint and she went to Ted about it. I remember thinking at the time that she was a bit extreme," Sandy said. "Like her husband."

"Whatever," I said, yawning loudly. "Look, this is all fascinating, but it's past my bedtime. Gunther has already claimed the pillow, and I need to get some sleep. Later, Sandy," I said, and hung up.

I was tired and keyed up at the same time. I closed my eyes, but couldn't stop all the thoughts that kept popping into my head. I kept picturing Henderson's body lying face down at the bottom of the pool.

On the pillow beside me, Gunther had lapsed into one of those deep cat sleeps, eyes screwed shut, whiskers and tail twitching involuntarily.

The phone rang about 10:40. Damn. I'd forgotten to unplug it. I had the feeling I should answer it.

"Jill, I hope you weren't asleep," Sandy said.

"No, I had to get up to answer the phone anyway," I replied.

"I thought you should know something Alice just told me," Sandy said.

"Oh, for Pete's Sake," I said. "I've already heard her wild ideas. She cornered me hours ago."

"Well, this is something new. Something she said

happened since she talked to you," Sandy said. "I'll put her on the phone. We're back in the kitchen," she said.

"Okay," I said reluctantly.

"Jill, is that you?" Alice asked in a small voice.

"Go ahead, Alice, I'm listening," I said, trying to sound patient.

"Well, after you left this morning, the sheriff asked me what all I had done in Dr. Henderson's room. I was the one assigned to it, you know. The one who was going to clean it for him while he was staying here. Well, I wasn't sure what the sheriff was asking me. It sounded like he was going to be mad at me, or something. I just told him that everyday when people go down to breakfast, that's when I start working on their rooms. Dr. Henderson's was the second one I did on Tuesday. I thought he must have been down at breakfast like everybody else. I didn't know anything about him swimming, you see. I told the sheriff that I changed the towels, and cleaned the bathroom. But I didn't say anything to him about the little bar of soap still being wrapped up, like I told you. I don't know why, I just felt like he was looking for an excuse to yell at me. So, I figured I shouldn't say any more than I had to."

"That's not right, Alice," I said. "You need to tell Sheriff Clark and the deputies everything. You haven't done anything to make him yell at you. He might though, if you withhold information from him," I said. Silence. "Alice? Alice, are you still there?" I asked.

"Yes," she said. "There's something else I didn't tell you before. I don't think Dr. Henderson slept in his bed."

"What do you mean?" I asked. "Where did he sleep?"

"No, that's not it. I mean, I don't think his bed was slept in. It's just like he tried to make it look like he had," she said.

"Look, Alice, that doesn't make any sense. Why on earth would he do that? I think your imagination is really running wild now. Do us all a favor, just forget all these crazy ideas you've got, okay?" I said loudly.

"I can't. It's not over, you see. Not with his wife coming here today. I got her room all ready for her. She's staying in the Executive Suite. I hope she likes it okay. But I heard she could be, you know, nasty. It happened the other time she was here. I wish I didn't have to be the one to have to clean her room this time. She was so horrible to Ellen, and complained to Ted about her, and got her fired."

"Really? Fired? Is that true, Alice?" I asked.

"Sure it is. Ellen's my friend. I still talk to her all

the time. She's working now at…."

I cut her off. "Alice," I said. "Listen, if you're scared of having to clean Mrs. Henderson's room, ask Ted to change the schedule. Give the room to somebody else."

"Oh, no! I can't talk to Ted! He's always so mean to me, too," she cried.

"All right. All right. Calm down," I said. "Do you remember what Ellen said was the problem when Mrs. H. was here before?"

"Let me think. Oh, right. Ellen said that when Mrs. Henderson was here before, she took care of her room, and she thought that two people used Mrs. Henderson's room the first night. But it was only booked as a single, you see. Mr. Henderson wasn't even here then. Ellen said she could tell two people had used the bathroom and the bed. I can always tell, too, you know. It's not hard. There are a lot of signs, if you know what to look for," she began

"Whoa, Alice. I don't need to know about that," I said. "Put Sandy back on, will you?"

After a moment, I heard Sandy's voice again. "What do you make of that?" she asked.

"Not much. I think she's been reading too many detective magazines. Look, I've really got to get some sleep. I'll call you later. Now I'm unplugging the phone," I said.

"Sweet dreams," Sandy said. "Oh, Jill? Are you still there?"

"Here," I said wearily.

"Pam and I had a long talk last night. We covered a lot of ground. About Keith and me. And about you and Mitch, too. I was telling her that you and Mitch were, you know, sort of on-again, off-again. I didn't think you'd mind," she said.

"No. Is there a point to this?" I asked.

"Well, for what it's worth, Pam said you'd be pretty foolish to let Mitch Garrett get away. She said she's always thought of him as one very special guy, and if it weren't for the fact that she was so madly in love with her husband, she might be interested in him herself," Sandy said.

"Thanks for the input. Tell Pam I'll let her know if we ever get around to picking out the silver pattern," I said, and hung up.

I still couldn't get to sleep. I found my thoughts going back to what Alice had said about Mrs. Henderson.

I tried to figure out a connection between Ellen's speculations about two people having been in the room and Mrs. Henderson having Ted fire her, if, in fact, that was what had happened.

Had Mrs. Henderson somehow overheard Ellen telling someone this piece of gossip? Was it really true? And was it worth having Ellen fired?

Then my thoughts went back to something else Alice had said. Something about the body. Oh, right. About Ricky and Warren saying that the body had been stiff when we pulled it out. Had it been? I searched my memory for the answer. Yes. It had. Based on everything I'd studied, rigor mortis usually occurs about two or three hours after the victim drowns. We pulled him out around 7:45. That means he would have gone into the water between 4:45 and 5:45 for his swim. In a way that seemed awfully early for a swim, but what did I know? Even if the body was stiff, as Alice was telling everyone, what did that mean? I forced myself to push all of Alice's ridiculous comments out of my head.

If I didn't get to sleep soon, I'd be worthless on the job tonight. I closed my eyes, and tried to breathe with the rhythm of Gunther's snoring. The phone jolted me awake at 11:15. I'd forgotten to unplug it again. Damn. Expecting it to be Alice with strike three, I grabbed the receiver, and barked, "This better be good!"

"It is, Jill," came Mitch's reply. "I thought you might already be asleep, but I've got something you ought to hear. Sheriff Clark just got off the phone with the coroner's office. Apparently, he's got some questions concerning Dr. Henderson's death. Sheriff Clark's calling Ted now to tell him to lock the room where Dr. Henderson stayed, not to let anyone in, and to close the pool until he can get down there to investigate."

I was nearly speechless. The full understanding of what Mitch was saying hit me. "Mitch, what do you think the coroner suspects? Or maybe I should just ask Alice. She may know more than all of us."

"What? Who's Alice?" Mitch asked.

"I'll tell you about that later. Let me give this some thought," I said. "Are you going back to the conference center with the sheriff to question people again?"

"Looks like it," Mitch said. "I'll know more when he gets off the phone with Ted. I'll keep you updated, Jill."

Mitch hung up, leaving me sitting on the edge of the bed fully awake. I padded into the kitchen and poured some milk. Sitting at the table, I tried to sort everything out. Was Mitch saying that the coroner did not believe that Dr. H. died as the result of an accident? If not an accident, what else could it be? It's pretty hard to commit suicide by drowning. And there's almost always a note. And why come all the way from Philadelphia to do it?

That only left murder. The word made be shiver. Who would want to murder Dr. H.? I hadn't even known the man. How could I try to figure out who would have wanted him dead? I was probably getting way ahead of myself here. Mitch had not said anything about murder.

For the third time that morning, the phone rang. I grabbed the receiver from the wall phone in the kitchen.

"Jill?" Sandy's voice was low, almost a whisper.

"Sandy? What's wrong? Why are you whispering?" I asked.

"I don't want anyone to hear me. I have to tell you about something that just happened here. Ted got a call from Sheriff Clark and said to alert everyone that he and Mitch will be questioning people again. Ted said the coroner thinks that maybe Dr. Henderson's death wasn't an accident."

"You're the second person to tell me that in fifteen minutes," I said. "Mitch just called."

"He did? What did he say?" Sandy asked.

I filled her in with the few additional details Mitch had given me.

"Well, Mrs. Henderson got here about an hour before the sheriff called. Ted had a phone call a few minutes before the taxi arrived, and Ted went over to the guest quarters to meet her. He carried her bags for her," Sandy said.

"So? I asked. "He's probably just knocking himself out to make things easier on her. I'm sure he's scared to death of a lawsuit.

"You may be right," Sandy said. "I'd better let

Dr. Thorpe know that Mrs. Henderson has arrived. I've got to go. I'm going to Pam's after work. Want to come over for a swim before your shift?"

"Maybe. I still need to get some sleep," I said, and hung up.

Chapter Ten

I must have fallen asleep around noon, and woke up at five o'clock, feeling like I hadn't even been to bed. I showered and dressed in my uniform, planning on going in to work as soon as Mitch called. I felt I needed to get to the conference center soon; that's where all the action was.

Gunther stood in front of his empty bowl, having worked up an appetite sleeping. I fed him and carved out some dinner for myself from the Entenmann's box on the counter. Gunther and I were sharing the last of the milk, when I heard a soft knock at the front door.

Mitch stood on the steps. "I wasn't sure you'd be awake," he said. "I guess I should have called first, but I have a lot to tell you and thought I'd better do it in person." He came in and we sat together at my kitchen table. Gunther settled under my chair and gave himself a thorough bath, pausing every so often in mid-lick to listen more closely to our conversation.

"Sheriff Clark and I just left Ted's office. We've been at the conference center all afternoon, interviewing people and searching Dr. Henderson's room. This has now become an official investigation, Jill," Mitch said. He looked as tired as I felt, and I wondered how we could keep up this relationship with our screwy schedules.

"Start at the beginning," I said. "What did the coroner find out?"

"Well, he said that Henderson did drown. He also said that there was a sizeable bump on his head. He thinks this may have happened right before he drowned. Possibly he hit his head on the edge of the pool, lost consciousness, and drowned," Mitch said.

"So?" I asked, not understanding what the coroner was questioning about this scenario. It seemed perfectly logical to me.

"He told the sheriff he believed the temperature of the cold water in the pool should have revived the doctor when he hit the water. And that he should have been able to manage to get himself to the side of the pool. But there was another detail that really made him wonder. Henderson apparently wore contact lenses. When the autopsy was done, he was only wearing one."

Again I said, "So? Don't some people only need

to wear one contact lens? Or what if one popped out when he hit his head? Or washed out in the pool… Oh, I see, he wouldn't have worn his lenses into the pool, or else he might lose them."

"Right," Mitch said. "We've learned today that most people who wear lenses leave them out when they swim, or wear goggles to keep from losing them in the water. So, he thinks it's really odd that he was wearing one lens when he went in swimming."

"I guess you've talked to his wife? Sandy said she arrived today from Philly," I said.

"Yes, we did talk to her. We asked her about her husband wearing contacts, and, at first, she didn't seem to know whether he kept them in while swimming. Then she remembered that he usually took them out," Mitch said. "We checked his toiletries bag—it's still in his room. There's a case for his lenses, but it's empty. If he went out for an early morning swim, he wouldn't have been wearing the lenses. Yet, he had one in and the other one is missing. So, it's pretty puzzling."

"And he didn't wear disposable lenses, either?" I asked, trying to offer other explanations.

"No, we thought of that. We got the name of his eye doctor from his wife, and checked it out. He wore a soft lens in each eye, and they were the kind that have to be removed every night. He was very nearsighted. He had a pair of glasses that he needed to use if he wasn't wearing the contacts. Based on what the eye doctor told us about Henderson's vision being so bad, he would have needed his glasses to get down to the pool. But his glasses were still up in his room."

"What does the sheriff think all this means?" I asked, feeling a sense of apprehension start in my stomach.

"That maybe his death was not accidental. That maybe someone gave him that bump on the head and put him in the pool to make it look like he drowned," Mitch said.

"But why?" I asked. "The man was here for a conference with a bunch of his colleagues. Who would have wanted to kill him? Did you tell his wife all this? What did she say?"

"We told her the facts as we have them, but nothing about our suspicions. We really don't have enough to build a case on just yet. We did ask her if she knew of anyone in her husband's life who might wish him harm. She was shocked that we were even thinking about anything like that. She said he had no enemies."

"I talked to Sandy this morning." I said. "She remembered Mrs. Henderson being at the conference center last year to attend a financial meeting. Apparently, there was some problem that she made a big stink about, and one of the housekeepers got fired because of it".

"Really? Are you sure? Ted told me yesterday morning that Kate Henderson had never been to the conference center before. No wait, maybe what he said was that he had never met her," Mitch said thoughtfully.

"Are you sure that's what he said? That he'd never met her?" I asked.

"I'll have to check my notes," Mitch said. "Is it important?"

"Well, that would really be strange," I said. "Because Alice told me that Mrs. H. bitched to Ted in person about the housekeeping problem and that's when he fired whoever was responsible. So it sounds to me like Ted does know the widow."

"Whoa, who's this Alice you keep bringing up?" asked Mitch, frowning. "Did I miss something?"

"Alice is one of the housekeepers there. She's kind of spooky, if you ask me. She lurks around and sneaks up on people," I said. "I've seen her dusting or straightening, and she looks like she's in another world, but apparently she's tuned in to everything that's going on around her. She's like a fly on the wall. You just don't notice her."

"Does this Alice remember anything else about the time Kate Henderson was there before? What the problem was, I mean?"

"Something about two people having stayed in Mrs. Henderson's room. And it wasn't Dr. Henderson," I said.

"Alice also has some pretty odd ideas about what she thinks did and didn't go on in Dr. Henderson's room in the last day or so," I said.

"Sounds like I'd better talk to Alice," Mitch said.

"She won't be here until early in the morning," I said. "Can it wait?"

"I'll see what Sheriff Clark wants me to do about it," Mitch said. "Are you going in to work now?" he asked, eyeing my uniform.

"I was, but Sandy invited me to come to Pam's for a swim. She's babysitting Pam's kids. I really feel like I want to bring her up to date on this. Want to come with me?" I asked.

"Sure. Why not?" Mitch said. "Let's take my car, and I'll bring you back here to get your truck later."

On the way, I told Mitch something I'd never told him before about Sandy. I suspected he may have heard it from Pam or Eddie, but I wanted to make sure he'd heard the story correctly.

Sandy and Keith had had a little girl named Emma, who had died when she was five. The pain of losing a child affects different people in different ways, I suppose. Instead of bringing Sandy and Keith closer together, Emma's death had driven a wedge between them. I don't know if either guilt or blame played a role; Emma had died from a virus. Sandy called the doctor as soon as Emma became sick, but by the time the doctor checked her into the hospital, it was very serious. After Emma died, Sandy tried to fill her time by taking the full-time job at the conference center—something Keith hated very much.

He didn't think it was a good reflection on him—his wife working. Apparently he made big bucks as a sales rep for some company, and they lived in a nice house in a nice community. But he traveled a lot, and Sandy couldn't stand spending so much time alone in the house. Mitch listened, but didn't respond.

I finished by saying that it had been a long time since Sandy had been able to be around her sister's children. The fact that she had recently started to babysit for them made me think that she was finally coming to terms with her loss.

As soon as we pulled up behind Sandy's car in the paved circular driveway, we could hear children's loud voices coming from the backyard swimming pool. We walked around the side of the one-story stone rancher and let ourselves in through the black wrought iron gate.

Cries of "Aunt Jill! Aunt Jill!" greeted us, as Hayley and Jack, aged five and six, quickly paddled for the steps at the shallow end. Although they'd learned to swim when they were toddlers, they wore bulky yellow life jackets.

"Hi, you two," Sandy said to us from the edge of the pool. They had mounted the steps and were hurrying toward us. "Now, kids, don't get them all wet, yet!" she said. "Get your towels. They're over there on the chair." But it was too late for that. Hayley was hugging me around my thighs, water seeping into my pants. Jack raised his arms to me, wanting to be picked up. I grabbed one of the beach towels from the chair and wrapped him in it, then scooped him into my arms. His small arms circled my neck and he kissed me on the cheek.

"How is everybody?" I asked.

Excited voices murmured their answers, and Sandy said, "Mitch, I'm so glad Jill invited you. It couldn't be any hotter, could it? We're supposed to get some relief Thursday, I think. And God knows, we need the rain. Why don't you two put on your suits and get cooled off? I'm just going to go in and get some clothes for these little guys."

"I haven't seen Pam or Eddie for a long time." Mitch said. "I was hoping one or both of them would be here."

"Sorry, neither one," Sandy said. "Eddie's trying to finish a job he's doing. They're putting a roof on a house, and with the threat of a storm in the next day or two, they want to get it finished. You know Eddie; he's the boss, but he'd still rather be up there on the roof hammering with his crew than sitting behind the desk. Pam's out running some errands. Maybe we can all get together some night soon. That would be fun, wouldn't it?" she said, as she headed for the back door.

Mitch and I changed in the pool house and jumped into the sparkling blue water. When Sandy came out with lemonade for everyone, we sat with her in the row of chaises.

Talk quickly turned to the latest news concerning the investigation into Dr. Henderson's death. Surprisingly, Mitch told Sandy everything that he had told me. He asked if she had heard any additional information from Alice, but she hadn't.

"Since we're not quite sure what we've got here, Sandy, I'd appreciate it if you didn't talk to anyone else about this," Mitch said. "This is an official investigation now. Of course, you can tell Keith."

"I appreciate your confidence in me, Mitch," Sandy said. "I certainly won't discuss it with anyone. Not even Keith. He doesn't like to hear about anything to do with my job. I haven't even told him about Dr. Henderson drowning."

"It's probably just as well," said Mitch, "considering how he feels about your working there."

"The only time we don't argue about it is when he's traveling. He's got a good job and he says he can buy us everything that we could possibly want. That's the only way he knows how to measure happiness anymore. I'll never to able to convince him that I work because I want to. Because I need to. Every time we talk about it, we cover the same ground," Sandy said. "We have so little left between us. We just live in the same house. That's what it comes down to. Keith's isolated himself from everyone we used to see. He has no outside interests any more, except for his work. When he is at home, he spends his time doing paperwork or watching sports on television. If I didn't have my job, and my family and friends, I don't know how I would manage. It took me a long time to realize how important Pam and her children are to me. It was just too painful to be around them for so long. I hope everyone understands that."

We sat in silence, watching the children play on the swing set, and sipping our lemonade. My thoughts turned back to the one word none of us had spoken. Did we have a murder on our hands?

Mitch said that he was anxious to talk to Alice in the morning, if that was what Sheriff Clark wanted him to do.

We talked about all the business of towels and soap that Alice had told us.

"They may be key pieces of evidence," Mitch said. "I wouldn't be too quick to discount what she's told you."

"Hey," I said suddenly. "Mitch, you didn't say anything about the time of death. What did the coroner say about that?"

"That's very difficult to determine. Based on the amount of rigor mortis, he can only be certain that death occurred sometime before 5 o'clock. It seems unlikely that the doctor would have gone for a swim that early." We sat in silence again, considering this information.

"What about Mrs. Henderson having Ellen fired?" Sandy asked. "Do you think there's any kind of connection there?"

"I don't see one at this point," Mitch said.

"It's time for me to get home and pick up my truck," I said to Mitch. "Thanks for the swim, Sandy. Tell Pam I'll see her later.

"Jill, the sheriff has authorized a deputy to be

on the premises of the conference center twenty-four hours a day until this thing's cleared up. When you get there, look for Don. He's pulling the overnight shift. I'll probably be there tomorrow night."

After that announcement, we drove back to my house in silence, alone in our thoughts, but undoubtedly having some of the same ones.

CHAPTER ELEVEN

It was a quiet Wednesday night. Both the temperature and humidity were unusually high for May, and my damp uniform clung to me. I'd seen Don as soon as I'd gotten there. He said he'd checked all the buildings and found nothing to report. I spent most of the night alternating talking to Deirdre and Alan, the only other two conference center employees who shared my shift. I hoped there'd be no need for me to have to leave the air-conditioned comfort of either desk.

When Sandy arrived for work Thursday morning, I met her in the parking lot. "What's going on?" she called from her car.

"Not a damn thing. Don's been on watch all night. Sheriff Clark and another deputy got here a few minutes ago. They're going to search Dr. Henderson's room again. And I think they'll be talking to our buddy, Alice, too."

"Oh, I feel sorry for her. She didn't tell the sheriff everything the first day he was here. Now she's going to have a lot of explaining to do," Sandy said, as we walked toward the conference center.

"Oh, for crying out loud, they're not going to torture her, you know. But maybe she needs a little shaking up," I said, impatiently. "She had information they could have used, but she decided to share it with us instead of them. That's not right."

"I know. But she's so vulnerable," Sandy said. "I hope she won't be upset that we've told Mitch so much of what she's told us."

"It would serve her right," I said. "For Pete's sake, it's a police investigation. We had to tell Mitch what we knew."

Alan was standing in the kitchen talking with Sheriff Clark when we walked into the lobby area. They both looked out at us through the doorway, and I heard the sheriff excuse himself.

"Morning, ladies," he said, touching the brim of his hat. "Ms. Pearce, I'd like to ask you a few more questions, if you've got a minute. You should probably stay for this, too, Miss McCormick."

"Of course," Sandy said. "I wish you'd call me Sandy, Sheriff."

"Yes, ma'am. Mitch tells me that you two ladies have told him quite a lot about Dr. and Mrs. Henderson. Some information you got from Alice, is it?" he said.

"Yes, that's right," I answered. "Alice has been telling us these little pieces of information since the morning that Dr. Henderson was found. It wasn't until I heard that the coroner thinks it may not have been an accident, that I thought there might be something to what she's been saying."

"You know for a fact that Kate Henderson has been here before?" he asked.

"Yes, sir, I do," said Sandy. "She was here for a conference. I'm not absolutely certain about when that was, but more than a year ago, I'm sure. I can check our files and let you know," she offered.

"Won't be necessary," he said. "You talked to her when she was here?"

"Well, I don't remember that I actually talked to her. I could have," she said.

"But you know she talked to Ted?"

"No, at one time I thought that was the case, but now I'm not positive about that either. Alice is the one who claims that she did," Sandy said.

"I see," he said. "So you can't actually say for a fact that Ted and Kate Henderson knew each other before this? You never saw them together."

"No, sir, I guess not," she said. "Not until yesterday when she arrived. Ted greeted her and carried her luggage."

"I see," he said. He looked out the window toward the guest building. "Think Alice is cleaning those rooms now?"

"Yes, sir, I would imagine she is," Sandy said. "If you'd like, I can page her to come here."

"Don't bother," he said. "I'll find her. Thanks." He touched the brim of his hat again and left through the back door.

Alan had gone without saying good-bye. Sandy checked the desk area for any messages. Finding none, she sat down at the desk. It was then she pointed out that the light for Ted's extension was lit up on the front desk phone. "This is really early for him to be in his office," she said.

"I didn't notice his car in the lot just now either. He certainly is here early," I said. "A lot going on, I suppose."

A young man with glasses and a neatly trimmed beard entered the lobby and approached the desk.

"Good morning," he said to Sandy. "Thank you for letting me know that Mrs. Henderson got here yesterday. I left a message with the attendant at the desk at the guest building that I would like to see her when it is convenient. She may come here looking for me sometime today. Would you be so kind as to come into the meeting room and get me, please?" he asked.

"Yes, sir," Sandy said. "Absolutely."

"I wish to be of service to her in any way possible. I would like to offer to take her wherever she needs to go to make arrangements for Dr. Henderson," he said.

"I understand, sir," Sandy said, and he went into the meeting room.

I heard all this while gazing out the window at the overcast day. The humidity hung in the air like a gauze curtain. The weather forecast promised relief by tonight in the way of severe thunderstorms.

I thought about Mrs. H. having to identify her husband's body and make arrangements for him to be returned to Philadelphia. She had probably already started planning his funeral. I was still having a difficult time believing that Dr. H. could have been murdered. I wondered if the authorities in Philadelphia were involved in the investigation on their end. I'd ask Mitch the next time I saw him.

"Well, good morning, girls," we heard a soft voice announce. Sandy and I looked up to see Claire Stewart coming down the staircase in the far corner of the lobby.

Claire was head of the Sales Department for the Chesapeake Conference Center, and her department took up most of the second floor.

Claire always dressed as the polished professional that she was. Her tailored skirt and jacket in a periwinkle blue complimented her dark coloring. Her accessories were small and tasteful, and her short, neat haircut gave the impression that this lady was prepared to handle just about anything that came her way.

Sandy has told me she admired Claire for the way she handles prospective clients when taking them on a tour of the facility. Claire is a knowledgeable and gracious representative of the conference center. She has a talent for giving her undivided attention to someone—for making him, or her, feel as though they are the only person in the world that she needs to work with at that moment.

In reality, Sandy said that Claire is one of the most overworked employees here. She often works late, and usually takes home a mound of paperwork on the weekends. The conference center is her whole life. It's criminal that Ted makes things so difficult for her. Our boss is the one aspect of the job that Claire can't control. But then again, I guess none of us really can.

"It certainly is typical Maryland summer weather today, isn't it? Hazy, hot, and humid. The only way we're going to shake this heat is to get a storm. God knows, we need the rain. But then we'll lose the power, and there go the computers. Oh, well." Claire said. "Goodness, Jill, I never get to see you. You're always gone by the time I get in. How come you're here so late?" Claire asked.

"A lot going on, as you know," I said. "How come you're here so early?" I asked her right back.

"Ted's invitation. I'm sure I don't know why he has to see me at this ungodly hour, but who am I to question him?" she said. "I probably should have worn my suit of armor, although with Ted's X-ray vision, it wouldn't have done any good."

"Claire, is that still going on?" Sandy asked. "I thought you said you talked to him. You know there are laws against the way he treats you."

"I know, I know. I did talk to him, but it didn't do any good. Whenever I'm anywhere near him, I just feel like he's undressing me with his eyes. I'm scared to say much more to him about it. You know what happened to Denise," she said, lowering her voice even more.

"Well, we don't know for a fact that Ted arranged for her to be transferred," Sandy said.

"Why are you giving that jerk the benefit of the doubt?" I asked. "I think someone could build a pretty good case that that's exactly what happened to her."

"I agree with Jill," Claire said. "But I don't think I want to pursue it. I need to keep my job. Look, I'd better get on in there and get this over."

"Call if you need help," I said, and Claire rolled her eyes.

"Oh, by the way," Claire said, dropping her

voice. "I wonder if either of you have heard anything about the story that Ted and his wife have separated," Sandy and I exchanged looks and shook our heads.

"I heard something about it a few weeks ago. Maureen down in the kitchen said that Ted's been living at the Bayshore Apartments for almost two months. Her sister-in-law or some relative of hers works in the rental office there. And last weekend, someone else said he saw Ted and a woman having dinner at the Candlelight Inn over in Annapolis. He'd seen Ted at the Christmas parties here with his wife, and the woman he was with in Annapolis didn't look like the same woman."

"I haven't heard anything like that, Claire," Sandy said.

"Neither have I," I said.

All three of us jumped at Ted's voice. "Claire, go on in to my office. I'll be right back," he said, and headed down the hall toward the men's room.

Claire paused a few seconds, buttoned her jacket up to her neck, took a deep breath, and went into Ted's office.

"Wow! What about that news?" I asked. "Ted and Mrs. Ted have split up."

"Claire said it's only a rumor. Let's not make any assumptions," Sandy said.

"Why are you always sticking up for that guy?"

I asked. "Especially when he treats you like crap."

"He is my boss, and I try to have some respect for him," she answered.

We both kept quiet when we heard Ted approaching. He stopped to admire himself in the large mirror in the lobby. He straightened his tie and smoothed his perfect blond hair. When he turned toward us, "Hold all my calls," was the only thing he said.

"I rest my case," I said, after he was out of earshot.

I stood up, preparing to leave for home, when the phone rang.

"Sandy Pearce…. Oh. Thank you, I'll let him know," she said, and hung up. "Mrs. Henderson is on her way over. I have to go tell Dr. Thorpe," she said, heading for the meeting room.

As soon as she came in, I knew I had never seen her before. I would have remembered. Her hair was cut in a severe, short style; the color, a platinum blonde. She wore a tight-fitting black coatdress that was very short on her tall, slim frame. Large stud earrings that had to be real diamonds were the only jewelry she wore. Her stiletto heels clicked as she walked over the metal threshold at the front door.

She paused in the doorway and, ignoring me, walked toward the meeting room. I remembered

Sandy saying that both Dr. Henderson and Dr. Thorpe worked at the same Philadelphia hospital. Their wives probably knew each other socially. Sandy and Dr. Thorpe were just coming through the meeting room door when the widow arrived. He gently embraced her, and gave her a small kiss on the cheek. They spoke in soft murmurs for a few minutes, then he walked her toward the desk, so I couldn't help but overhear their conversation.

"So you are quite sure that there is nothing that I can do to help you, dear lady?" he said.

"No, thank you, you're so kind. Mr. Savin, the manager, insists on taking me himself this afternoon to go into town. And I'll be driving Roger's car back later today. I came down to Baltimore on the train yesterday and took a cab here."

"I see. Well, if you're sure there's nothing that I can do? And you will let us know all the details the minute the arrangements are final, won't you?" Dr. Thorpe asked.

"Of course," she answered with a smile. After a final embrace, she went out through the front door, and he returned to his meeting.

As Sandy sat down, I stood again, this time determined to go home to my bed. I heard the back door open and peered down the hallway, trying to see if it might be the sheriff with more questions.

I was surprised to see Alice hurrying up to the desk. She was nearly out of breath and collapsed into the chair next to mine. "Gosh, I'm so upset," she said. "The sheriff came to talk to me this morning. He confused me so much. Sandy, I needed to talk to you, but I couldn't get away until I'd finished cleaning all my rooms, you see, or I'd have come right over. But I need to ask you something. When Mrs. Henderson was here before, didn't you see her talking to Ted? About Ellen, I mean?"

"No, Alice, I never saw them together. You said that you did, though," I answered.

"Well, the sheriff is saying that I must be wrong. He says that Ted is sure that Mrs. Henderson never talked to him when she was here before. I don't get it. I know that's what I heard back when it happened. And I know that Ellen told me that Ted called her into his office and Mrs. Henderson was standing right there, and that's when he fired her. They didn't even give her a chance to explain her side of it or anything. Ellen said it was like they ganged up on her. He just said that because of what Mrs. Henderson had told him, he had to fire her, and that was that."

"Alice, it was a pretty long time ago. Maybe you're not remembering exactly what Ellen told you at the time," I said. "Why would Ted say one thing and Ellen say another?"

"Well, that's what I kept thinking," Alice said, still a little breathless. "And that's why I called Ellen last night. To make sure, you see. And she told me everything that happened that day. And she says that Ted and Mrs. Henderson were right there together in his office when she got fired. And I believe Ellen."

We all turned at the sound of Ted's door opening. Moving remarkably quickly, Alice darted into the kitchen for refuge. Ted marched out the front door, without a word to anyone. In the few seconds that the door was open, we heard distant thunder. A moment later Claire emerged from Ted's office, eyes fixed forward, and walked to the stairway. Her face was an unbecoming shade of anger.

"Poor Claire," Sandy said. "I'd better call her ."

As she reached for the receiver, I headed for the back door. "I'm going home to my bed. Gunther will be starting to worry," I said.

After the long drive home, I fell asleep in record time and didn't stir until just before Mitch knocked on the door at seven o'clock that night.

CHAPTER TWELVE

Mitch gently placed his hands on either side of my face and leaned toward me until our lips touched. My eyes closed and I could feel the heat of his body. It was a long, thorough kiss. The kind that Mitch does so well.

We parted a few inches, and his eyes locked on mine. He slowly removed his equipment belt and without looking, carefully placed it on the dresser next to where he stood.

Still looking at me, he pulled his shirttail out of his pants, and began undoing the buttons. He removed it, letting it fall to the floor. He pulled his tee shirt off over his head, and let that fall, too. I rested my hands on his exposed chest and let them lightly drift down toward his waist. Closing his eyes, he leaned down to kiss me again.

I felt him slipping my robe from my shoulders, and I let my arms drop by my sides, so that the robe fell to the floor. In one smooth motion, Mitch lifted me into his arms and placed me on the unmade bed. From the corner of my eye, I could see Gunther watching discreetly from the windowsill.

* * *

Mitch had turned the volume on the patrol car radio low enough so that we could talk. Instead we rode in silence to the Copper Kettle, his hand holding mine on the seat beside his thigh. He gently stroked my knuckles with his thumb, and his mouth was wearing a slight grin.

The intense storm that had happened while we were in bed had dumped a great deal of rain in a short period of time, and there were many large areas of standing water in the roads. To the west were still a lot of dark clouds, promising more rain. Mitch switched off the wipers.

"Do you realize neither of us has said more than a few words for the past hour?" I asked.

"We didn't have to," Mitch said, his grin turning into a wide smile.

"No, I guess not," I said, smiling back at him. "Is it okay to talk now? I mean, I want to ask you about some things."

"Sure," he said, giving my hand a final squeeze before releasing it. I felt a shift in the atmosphere inside the car. Mitch wasn't good at combining business with pleasure.

"Did anyone search Dr. Henderson's room again

today? And has anyone found his missing contact lens?" I asked.

"Yes and no," he said. "The room's been searched, but the lens hasn't been found. It could be anywhere. There's a lot of territory to cover between that room and the pool. We're looking for something that's about the size of a dime and it's clear plastic. And with the heavy rains we've had, if it had been outdoors, it likely washed away."

"Even if you find it, what's that going to prove?"

"The way I see it, if for some reason the doctor did go into the pool with his contacts, and hit his head, the missing lens is probably near the pool. Or even still in the pool. If somebody hit him and put him in the pool and drowned him, the lens might still be in the location where he was hit," Mitch said. "If we find it, say, in his room, it would make a stronger case that somebody hit him there and then moved him. That somebody tried to make it look like he drowned."

"But that still won't tell you who did it or why," I said.

"That's true," he said. "You know all about motive, means, and opportunity, right? Well, we still don't have any motive either. The authorities in the town where the Hendersons live are working on it from their end, but so far, nothing.

They didn't seem to think they would find anything, either. The guy was a prince."

"And Mrs. H. wasn't any help?" I asked. "You couldn't pick up on any marital trouble between them, could you?"

"Not really," he said. "She didn't say all that much when we talked to her. Still seemed in shock, I guess. She told us they've been married twelve years, no kids. Both dedicated to their careers, both travel a lot. It's just hard to know where this thing is going," he said.

The Copper Kettle wasn't too crowded at this late dinner hour, and we got a parking space close to the door. We slid into a booth at the back and Rose took our order, returning to bring us tall glasses of iced tea. I didn't see Penny.

"I've been thinking about something, Mitch," I said. "It seems to me that a lot of attention has been given to establishing the fact that there is no one who can honestly say that Ted Savin and Kate Henderson knew each other before her husband died. Why do you think that is so important?"

"It does seem like the sheriff has been trying to nail that down during his line of questioning, doesn't it?" Mitch said. "But I don't know what to make of it."

"I know he talked to Sandy and Alice about it.

It was almost as if he were daring them to say it was so," I said.

"So, as far as we know, there isn't anyone who can actually swear that Ted and Henderson's wife knew each other before this week?" Mitch said.

Rose brought our plates, and refilled our iced tea.

"Wait!" I said. "There's still Ellen. She's the housekeeper who got fired when Mrs. Henderson was here the first time. She told Alice just the other night that she's absolutely sure that both of them were in Ted's office when she was fired. And there's still the question of why Ellen got fired," I said. "Has anyone from the Sheriff's Department talked to her yet?"

Wiping his mouth, Mitch said, "I told Sheriff Clark about Ellen, but whether or not he's done anything about contacting her, I don't know."

"Mitch, how close are Ted and the sheriff?" I asked, buttering my bread. After a few beats of silence, I looked up to see him staring at me, his full fork in midair. "Well, come on, for Pete's sake, isn't that what we're thinking?" I said, taking a bite.

"Be careful, Jill," Mitch warned. "Do you know what you're implying?"

"Of course, I do," I said. "We know that Ted and Mrs. H. have known each other for quite a while, because we have a witness named Ellen. And it looks like the sheriff is trying to keep our boy, Ted, from seeming like he's involved in this mess in any way. You talked about motive before, Mitch. I'll bet if we thought about it real hard, we could come up with something," I said sarcastically.

Mitch was leaning back in the booth, hands folded behind his head, staring at the ceiling. I knew that this was his deep thinking posture, and I also knew it was a good time to keep quiet.

After a few minutes, Mitch cleared his throat and said, "I'm not saying that you're right or wrong, Jill. But, this is my boss and your boss we're talking about here. We've got to be very careful. I can't very well go over Sheriff's Clark's head, now, can I?"

"What if you contacted the police in Philadelphia and said that you needed them to look into Mrs. Henderson's background, too? You're a deputy working on this case. You could do that without having to go through the sheriff, couldn't you?" I suggested.

Mitch considered this for a moment. "I don't see why not," he said.

"And what about talking to Ellen?" I said. "If you get the feeling that the sheriff may not want to bring her into this, for whatever reason, couldn't you go talk to her yourself? That wouldn't seem out of line either, would it?"

Mitch didn't have to think as long about this one. "No," he simply said.

Rose slid the check near Mitch's plate and asked if we wanted dessert. We shook our heads.

Driving back to my house, Mitch said, "I'm going to pull a shift tonight at the conference center. The sheriff wants us covering the place until we know what we've got here. I've got to stop by the station first, but I should see you before midnight. Don will be there with you until then."

He stopped his patrol car at the end of my driveway, and leaned over to give me a kiss that told me he'd rather go back inside to my unmade bed.

CHAPTER THIRTEEN

I drove into work under a sky that threatened to open up at any minute. The first thunder I heard was close by. I noticed Don's patrol car down near the kitchen. I parked close to the conference building, and hurried inside.

"Hey, Alan, how's it going tonight?" I asked.

"Quiet. We lost the power at home for a while this afternoon during that thunderstorm. Was it bad at your place?" he said.

"I don't remember," I said, a faint smile on my lips.

"Well, it was bad there. Of course, the storms are always stronger here where they come in right off the Bay. They lose some of their bite as they head east," Alan said.

He took an incoming call while I checked the windows and doors in the conference room. When I returned to the desk, he said, "Jill, could you do me a big favor? Deirdre says she's got a package at the Registration Desk that needs to be brought over here. It's something for the group's meeting tomorrow, and I need to set it up tonight. I'm expecting a call now or I'd run over there myself. Do you think you could get it for me sometime during your rounds tonight? I'd sure appreciate it."

"No problem," I said, grateful for something a little out of the ordinary. "I'm heading over there now anyway. I'll try to get back before the next storm."

I grabbed one of the large umbrellas hanging by the back door, and stepped out into the night. The humidity was heavy in the air, but the wind was beginning to pick up, and the leaves on the trees sounded restless.

The parking lot at the rear of the guest building was still full of the doctors' sedans. I entered the building through the heavy glass door and nodded to one of the housekeepers who was vacuuming the hallway in the downstairs guest wing. I didn't see anyone at the desk or in the small office off the lobby. I found the package on the counter, flagged with a yellow sticky note that said, "Take to Conference Building."

A loud rolling wave of thunder jolted me, and the lights flickered. I tucked the box under my arm, and headed quickly down the hallway. Just as my hand turned the doorknob, the skies opened up, and I quickly stepped back into the building. Before the door closed, I caught the scent of the first fat drops of rain hitting the hot blacktop. Steam rose from its surface, and in a matter of seconds, the rain was running off the pavement in streams. The wind drove the rain against the glass door, blurring my view. Lightning split the sky and thunder rolled heavily overhead. If only I'd come five minutes sooner, I could have made it back to the conference building before the storm broke. Well, I'd just wait it out for a little while. Hopefully, this downpour wouldn't last long. I had the umbrella, and could manage if the wind died down a bit.

The lights flickered once, then twice, then remained on. I heard the vacuum cleaner cutting off, then on, then off, then on again. Still looking out the door, I saw Ted's black sedan pull into the parking space nearest the door. The car's wipers were swiping at the windshield at their fastest speed, and the headlights made the rain look like a solid sheet of water. I could see two people in the front seat of the car. Ted's passenger was a woman. They sat for a moment, with the car's engine running and the wipers flicking furiously back and forth. I didn't think they could see me, but something made me take a step back. I watched as Ted leaned very close to the woman for just a split second. Then they parted, and the passenger door opened a few inches. The woman unfolded a newspaper and held it over her head as she emerged from the car. Without looking at Ted, she closed the door with her hip and ran toward the building.

I turned and quickly took several steps down the hall, stopping just in front of the door to one of the guest rooms. I faced the door and raised the package in my hand, as though reading the information on it. Just as she yanked open the glass door, a loud clap of thunder sounded, causing me to jump. I looked in her direction and nodded as she hurried by me, shaking out her newspaper.

I waited until she had gotten on the elevator before I went back to the glass door. I peered out into the gloom, to make sure Ted's car was gone. Opening the umbrella, I stepped out into the downpour. The wind continued to drive the heavy rain, and by the time I reached the shelter of the conference building's back porch, I was completely soaked. Juggling the umbrella and the box, I awkwardly unlocked the back door and hurried inside. I stood just inside the entrance, letting water drip off me and the umbrella, trying to convince myself that I had not just seen Ted kiss Mrs. Henderson.

CHAPTER FOURTEEN

I set the box down on the desk. Still speaking into the receiver, Alan nodded and handed me a small piece of paper. "Call Sandy @ home ASAP," it said.

I went back into the supply room and found some bath towels. In the ladies' room, I dried off my face and hair, and tried to blot my clothes. The damage wasn't as bad as I thought, and decided I would survive. But keeping my hands busy did not keep my mind from replaying the scene I'd just witnessed between Ted and the widow. I was anxious to talk to Mitch. But the message from Sandy concerned me even more.

I let myself into the conference room and turned on only the far row of overhead lights. I used the phone on the desk in the corner of the room and punched in Sandy's number. I was beginning to worry when she finally answered on the ninth ring.

"Are you okay?" I asked quickly.

"Better," she said. "Is this a bad time for you?

Can you talk?"

"Of course. Tell me what's happened," I said.

"Keith and I had a horrible fight. He suggested I leave," she said.

"For good?" I asked

"I—I don't know. He was angry at first, but then after he calmed down, said he thought it might be better if I go to stay at Pam's. I think he may be right." I heard her let out a big sigh before she continued. "It all started when he got home and wanted to know why I hadn't told him about Dr. Henderson's drowning. He'd heard it from someone he had a business lunch with today, and he said it made him look stupid not knowing anything about it. The man he talked to said that the police are investigating it as a murder. Jill, is that true?" Sandy asked, her voice shaking a little.

"Mitch has never used that word," I said. "Go on. What happened with you and Keith?"

"I said the reason I hadn't told him was because I'd knew he'd overreact and that it would end up in another big fight, just like it always does," Sandy said. "Then he asked me if it was true, if there had been a murder. I only told him a little bit about what you and Mitch and I talked about. I didn't want to give him any more ammunition than he already had. He got really angry at that point, and demanded, positively demanded that I quit my job."

I heard her voice crack and I said, "This is just the kind of excuse he's been waiting for. I'll bet he was really pushing you hard, wasn't he?" I asked.

"This is the angriest I've ever seen him about my job. It really scared me, Jill," she said. "Then he accused you of not doing your job. He said it should have been your responsibility to save the man from drowning."

"Hey, you don't need to give me another reason not to like your husband, Sandy," I said, my blood pressure rising. "What does he think I am, a lifeguard?"

"He called you a 'wannabe cop'" she said.

"Not that I care what he thinks, but what did you tell him about where I was?" I asked.

"I said that you were busy doing some paperwork for Ted in the conference building at the time the doctor drowned, and that you weren't anywhere near the pool," Sandy said.

"Well, that's the truth," I said.

"I know it is," Sandy said. "But Keith isn't interested in hearing the truth. He demanded that I quit my job, or else.

"Can I ask what 'or else' means?" I said.

"He didn't say. He just said that he had put up with my crap for long enough. That he never thought I should be working at all because it made him look bad. And now he hears that a murder may have been committed there."

"Boy, I bet he was furious," I said.

"I told him that if there had been a murder, the authorities will catch whoever did it, and that I didn't feel as though I were in any danger. Whatever the motive for the murder was, it wouldn't have anything to do with me or anyone else who works there," Sandy said.

"I told him that I needed my job. I needed someplace to go everyday. Someplace where I can perform a service that is needed. He said 'someplace where you won't be reminded that you don't have a family to take care of? Someplace where you won't always be thinking about the fact that you don't have a daughter anymore?'"

"That must have hurt like hell, Sandy," I said. "What did you say to him?"

"I told him there was no such place," she said. "Then I tried to explain to him that if he doesn't like me working, it's his problem, not mine, and that I intend to keep that job. That's when he said I should leave. He said he didn't really think of this house as a home anymore. Maybe he's right about that, too."

"I'm so sorry, Sandy. You know I've never really been too crazy about Keith. I'm just sorry you had to go through all that. Can I do anything? Like shoot the guy for you?" I asked.

I heard her laugh a little. "No, but thanks for offering," she said. "I think I will go to Pam's for a few days. Maybe when this whole drowning matter is cleared up, things will be better between us. What do you think, Jill?"

"You don't really want me to answer that, do you?" I said.

"I guess I already know your answer," she said. "I haven't been able to stop thinking about what he said about you not preventing the drowning. I've been thinking—you don't suppose that Ted deliberately kept you busy that night, do you?" she asked.

"What? Why would he do that?" I asked.

"Maybe to keep you from seeing something? I don't really know what I'm getting at. It's really just an odd feeling I've got about all this business," she said.

"Speaking of odd feelings," I said, and told her the scene I had witnessed between Ted and Mrs. H. in his car.

"Have you told Mitch?" she asked.

"I'm going to call him when we hang up," I said.

"What if Ted and Mrs. Henderson met when she was there for her financial meeting the year before last? What if they had some sort of attraction for each other then and followed up on it? What if they've had an affair since then? Philadelphia is less than 100 miles away from here. They could have met somewhere in between, then they'd each have less than an hour's drive.

"Maybe Ted's wife found out about the affair, and that's why they're separated. What if Ted killed her husband out of jealousy? No, it would be the other way around. Dr. Henderson could have found out about the affair and might have tried to kill Ted. But it was Dr. Henderson who died," Sandy said.

"Do you think Mrs. H. killed her husband?" I asked. I couldn't imagine a woman overpowering a man and killing him. "What if Ted had helped her? What if they did it together?"

There was silence on the line between us for a moment, each of us imagining possible scenarios. Then I remembered a crucial piece of evidence. "Mrs. Henderson knew that her husband wore contact lenses and she would have known that he didn't wear them when he went swimming. If she and Ted had staged it to look like an accidental drowning, wouldn't she have taken his lenses out to make it look as real as possible?" I asked.

"Maybe in such a state of panic, she didn't even give it a thought," Sandy said.

"At dinner tonight, I asked Mitch if he thought the sheriff was covering up for Ted. I mean, face it, Lyndon Clark really seems to be looking out for his old buddy, Ted, doesn't he?" I said.

"How could we ever prove that?" Sandy asked. "What did Mitch say?"

"He told me to be careful," I said.

"He's right, Jill," Sandy said, and hung up.

I checked my watch. 12:30. Friday. What a week it had been. Hopefully Mitch was here by now. Turning off the lights, I shut the conference room door, and headed for the desk.

"Thanks for getting that box, Jill. Did you call Sandy back? She sure sounded upset," Alan said.

"Yeah, I talked to her. She's okay." I heard the back door open and looked down the hall to see Alice heading my way, carrying her caddy of cleaning supplies. She caught sight of Alan at the desk, stopped, and beckoned me to come to her. I followed her down the hall, where she stopped in front of the ladies' room. She propped open the door with a wedge of black rubber, and set her caddy on the counter next to the sink.

"Something else," she said, as if we had just been having a conversation two minutes earlier. "The rug in the elevator was wet on Tuesday morning. Is it important?"

I stared at her, unsure what I was supposed to be thinking. "Why are you telling me?"

"Well, I'm not talking to the sheriff or any of those deputies any more. They're scaring me," she said, eyes very wide behind her thick glasses. "Will you tell somebody for me?"

"No, you've got to do it yourself, Alice. Grow up, will you?" I said.

"It wasn't even me that saw it," she said defensively. "It was Becky. She just told me this morning. I guess she didn't think anything about it until all this talk about him being murdered. She said that she remembers the rug on the elevator must have been wet, because she parked the vacuum on the spot right inside the door, right next to the buttons, where most people would stand, and when she pushed the vacuum off, the wheels left big wet dirty streaks on the rug in the upstairs hall. She had to clean it all up," Alice said.

"Look, Mitch will be here in a few minutes. He's a nice guy. Just tell him what you told me," I said. "He might even want to talk to Becky instead. Will she be here in the morning?"

"Yeah. She'll be here until one. She's got a dentist appointment this afternoon, but she won't be coming back here after that," Alice said, sounding relieved.

I left Alice in the bathroom, and went out the back door to find Mitch.

CHAPTER FIFTEEN

I could see both patrol cars down near the kitchen, Mitch and Don standing in conversation under a security light.

As I approached, Don was getting into his car, and signaled me with a wave of his hand.

I told Mitch the latest news from Alice. "Okay," he said. "I'll check it out. I'll find Becky when she comes in. What time does Ted usually get in?"

"Sometime between eight and nine, I guess. But sometimes earlier. Why?"

"I've had an idea," he said. "I'm going to ask him for Ellen's home address and phone number. Say I want to talk to her. I want to see his reaction."

"That's a great idea. But, what if he says he doesn't have the information? It's been a year and a half since she was fired. Sandy's probably got Ellen's address at the front desk," I said.

"It doesn't really matter where I get the information," he said. "Because it's Ted's reaction that's really going to tell us a lot."

"True," I agreed. "Did you tell Sheriff Clark about Ellen being able to verify that Ted and Mrs. Henderson knew each other that long ago?"

"Yes, I talked to him a while ago. He said he was going to ride out and talk to her. He already knew where she lived." Mitch and I locked eyes for a few seconds, but let our mutual thought go unspoken.

"I'll be glad when this thing's wrapped up," Mitch said. "I've still got a desk full of work back at the station. There are other crimes being committed, you know."

"Oh, and I thought you liked to spend time with me," I said, trying to look hurt.

"You know I do," he said, giving my shoulder a squeeze. "Oh, I almost forgot to tell you. I talked to the Philadelphia police sergeant who ran the background check on Dr. Henderson. While he was finding out what a wonderful person the doc was, he wasn't hearing the same thing about Kate Henderson. A lot of people told him the same story—the doctor wouldn't give his wife the divorce she wanted. Seems their marriage had been over for a long time, and they had just stayed married. But then apparently Kate had found a boyfriend and wanted a divorce. The sergeant told me that he's never amazed at how people love to gossip about people they know."

"What if it's not gossip? Couldn't that be the motive for Dr. Henderson's murder?" I asked quickly.

"Well, before you go down that road, I should tell you that Kate Henderson's got an alibi for Monday night," Mitch said. "She said she was at a weekend conference at a Washington, D.C. hotel. And her story checks out."

We stood there, silent for a moment, disappointed that we were no closer to the answers we sought.

Then I said, "Does Ted have an alibi?"

Mitch said softly, "I don't think he was ever asked to provide one." More silence, as we considered that.

Mitch and I walked the grounds for most of the night, sometimes together, sometimes separately. When our paths crossed, we'd share new theories with each other about the case. Around five o'clock, we sat on the dining room porch, and I told him about a decision I had made.

"You know, Mitch, maybe you shouldn't be the one to talk to Ellen. I mean, if she's anything like Alice, she's probably scared to death of the police, especially if Sheriff Clark has already talked to her. If he worked her over like he did Alice, she'd probably clam right up if you tried to talk to her."

"You may be right," he said. "But what are our

other options?"

"What if I talked to her?" I asked.

"I don't think she'd understand how you could be authorized to question her. No offense, but you're local security just here on these premises," Mitch said.

"Yeah, I know that. But, what if I didn't even say I worked here? This Ellen person has never met me and I sure as hell couldn't pick her out of a lineup. I'll just come up with some other reason to go talk to her and work in the doctor's death. Bridgewood's a small town, you know. What else is there to talk about around here?" I said.

"You will be careful, won't you?" he asked.

"Of course," I said. "Now I'm going to go down and check on Sandy. She had a rough night." As we walked down the gravel path, I gave Mitch a brief summary of the fight Sandy and Keith had. He listened, concern on his face.

"That's tough," he said. "Sandy's too sweet to have to put up with that crap."

"So, I'm going to make sure she's okay," I said. "Will you come over later? You know where the key is."

"Sure," he said, giving me a warm grin. "I'm going to stick around and see if I can get Ellen's address from Ted when he comes in."

I was grateful that the rain had stopped. There

had been showers off and on all night, just enough to put me in a bad mood. I saw the low, gray clouds far to the west, and figured we'd probably get another thunderstorm before nightfall.

Sandy was in the kitchen, fixing fresh coffee. Her eyes were red, but she gave me a big smile.

"You okay?" I asked.

"Sure. Don't worry. It will all work out. One way or another," she said. "I'll be at Pam's as of tonight."

I told her about my plan to go to Ellen's to see if I could learn any more about her and Kate Henderson. Sandy looked up Ellen's address in her file.

Chapter Sixteen

I found the address Sandy had given me. It was in a tidy little trailer park about fifteen minutes from the conference center. The trailers were surrounded on three sides by cornfields in their early stages. I figured in another month, the residents would be just about cut off from the rest of the world by corn stalks.

I passed the road leading into the park, and pulled my truck off on a deserted dirt lane. Quickly I changed from my work uniform into a black tee shirt and cutoff jeans that were in the back of the cab. I stuck my trousers and shirt with the Chesapeake Conference Center logo on it under the front seat. I traded my thick-soled work boots for sandals, trying to rub off the indentation that had been left on my calves by my socks. Feeling pleased with my disguise, I backed the truck out onto the paved road again.

Finding the house number, I parked on a small gravel parking pad next to a pretty beaten- up Camaro. The windows of the trailer were closed, even though it was very hot and muggy, and I could hear the hum of an air conditioner. With the homes so close to each other, I couldn't be sure if it was Ellen's AC or someone else's I was hearing. The only other noise was coming from a few lots down where I could see two little kids running through the spray of a lawn sprinkler.

I caught some motion out of the corner of my eye, and saw the door of the trailer across the street opening. I watched as an elderly woman cautiously made her way down the three concrete steps to the small patch of grass in her front yard. It was then that I noticed an old mixed-breed dog stirring from its nap under a picnic table in the old woman's yard. The dog rose to its feet slowly and stretched with great difficulty. It set its tail to wagging and waddled over to meet the old woman, who was waiting for the dog, her right hand extended out toward it. The pair made their way toward my truck, and I got out to greet them.

"You a friend of Ellen's?" she asked. "Don't remember seeing you before. Work with her, do you?"

Since I didn't have a story of my own, it seemed like this one might do. "Yes," I answered, smiling.

"I'm Jamie," I lied.

"WHO?" she shouted, cupping her hand to her ear. The dog woofed loudly, too, obviously as hard of hearing as its owner.

"JAMIE," I shouted back.

"Ellen ain't home now," she said in a bit quieter voice. "Haven't seen her since late yesterday afternoon." The dog confirmed this with another woof.

"You don't know where she's gone?" I asked, raising my voice.

"No, but I'd say she left in a hurry. Wash is still on the line, " she said, nodding toward Ellen's side yard. For the first time I noticed the few pieces of soaked clothing clipped to a short length of rope that was stretched between Ellen's trailer and her neighbor's. Even if the clothes had dried yesterday, last night's rain had given them another good soaking. Suddenly I was having doubts about my ability to play detective. Even the dog had probably noticed the wash on the line.

Warming to the conversation, I asked, "Is this her car?" I gestured toward the Camaro. She looked at me as if I had three heads. Oops, if I worked with Ellen, I'd probably know that, wouldn't I? I quickly added, "I mean, I know she didn't take her car. Did you see who picked her up?"

"No. I was watching that stupid game show on

TV, and I had the sound up kinda loud. I musta dozed off, cause the next thing I heard was a couple of car doors bang shut, and then it just roared out of here. Even I could hear that racket."

"But you didn't see anything? Could you tell if it was a car or a truck?" I asked.

"Nope." She answered simply. The dog lay down at her feet, bored with the conversation. It sniffed the heavy air and panted, it's tongue pulsing in and out of its mouth. I was trying to think of what else I could possibly learn from her, when she said, "This all happened not long after the sheriff was here."

This information jolted me, and I asked, "Was it actually Sheriff Lyndon Clark who was here, or one of the deputies from the sheriff's office? Did you see?"

"Course I saw. It was Lyndon. Known him for years, you know. His wife and me used to go to the same church," she added.

"What time was this? Do you remember? You said you were watching a game show on TV?" I asked eagerly.

"Beats me," she said. She looked thoughtfully at the dog, as if it might raise its head and supply the answer. "Maybe seven. Maybe eight. Not real dark out."

I couldn't think of anything else to ask, so I leaned

down and patted the dog. I thanked her for her time, raising my voice a bit. She nodded, and turned toward her trailer. Just before I started the engine, she called out, "When I see Ellen I'll tell her you was here. What'd you say your name was?" It was my turn to be deaf, so I just waved my hand as I started the engine, put it in first gear, and drove off.

Driving to my house, I had the horrible feeling that I might never get to meet Ellen. It would be asking too much to hope that her sudden disappearance was some kind of a coincidence. How could I find out where Ellen had gone and why? I felt as if I'd failed at my mission. But if Mitch had gone there, he would have come away empty-handed, too. And his patrol car might have kept that lady and her dog out of sight, too. So maybe I had come out ahead.

Seeing Mitch's car in my driveway had always made me feel safe. But now I wasn't getting the same feeling of comfort. I didn't have any problem believing that Ted was probably guilty as hell of something, but it was really gnawing at me that Sheriff Clark was somehow mixed up in this mess, too. I pulled in behind Mitch's car and let myself in the kitchen door.

Mitch had closed all the window shades and even though it was only ten o'clock in the morning, the living room looked as it does at dusk. He was half sitting, half lying on the sofa, boots off, with his eyes closed. Gunther was curled up on the cushion next to Mitch. I saw Mitch's gun belt and two-way radio on the TV cabinet. I went into the kitchen to see what I could do about feeding all of us. Gunther soon appeared at my feet and wolfed down the plate of dry food I put on the floor for him. What did I want to eat? Breakfast or lunch?

As I bent to search the contents of the refrigerator, the cold air reaching my bare legs, I felt Mitch's arms circle my waist from behind. I stood up, and he brushed my hair over to one side, and gently kissed the back of my neck. I pushed the refrigerator door closed, forgetting what it was I wanted to get out of there.

I slowly turned to face Mitch. His arms were still around me and he gently pressed against me, tighter and tighter, until we were touching in all the right places. I kicked off my sandals and pulled my tee shirt off over my head. He took my hands in his, and staring into my eyes, led me down the hall. I saw Gunther in the kitchen, standing at his food bowl, looking relieved that I had fed him first.

* * *

As I finished putting the last of the dishes in the drainer, Mitch told me about Ted's reaction when he asked for Ellen's address.

"Ted may have made a little mistake. He said something about the sheriff having already talked to her, and that I shouldn't need to see her, too," Mitch said. "But then he located the address and wrote it down for me, making sure to give me the phone number, too. He seemed to be going out of his way to be helpful. "I'm not sure what kind of reaction I was looking for, but he just didn't seem sincere."

Then I told Mitch about my encounter at Ellen's trailer park. He was silent, leaning back in his chair at the kitchen table, staring at the ceiling. I knew to keep quiet. I wiped the stove and rinsed Gunther's dish, and went into the living room to wait for Deputy Garrett to share his thoughts with me.

"I agree with you that Ted's implicated in the murder," he said a few minutes later, joining me on the sofa. "At least as an accessory. If Kate Henderson actually did kill her husband, Ted has to have known about it, and in all probability, helped her. But, I don't know about Sheriff Clark. What's his stake in all this? He's a friend of Ted's, but a good enough friend to help Ted cover up his involvement in a murder? I can't really see that being the case. He's my boss, and up until right now, I have always respected him, so maybe I don't want to see it. I don't think I can be objective about him."

"Well, I can, and I say he's guilty. Maybe he didn't help with the murder, but he's guilty of something. Guilt by association. Is that a crime?" I asked.

Mitch chuckled. "I don't think so. We don't have much proof that anyone's guilty at this point. The investigation's at a standstill. Kate Henderson has an alibi. We don't know if Ted has one. Should I suggest to Sheriff Clark that he ask Ted if he has one? That could really make this whole thing blow up in our faces. If there was only some way that we could catch Ted and Lyndon at something that would tell us that they are definitely mixed up in this together. But I don't know how we can do that."

"What about if we try to figure out how Dr. Henderson was murdered?" I suggested. "Try and put ourselves in the murderer's place, and see how it works out. It may help us fit in some of these puzzle pieces that we've got lying around."

"Okay. It's worth a try," Mitch said. "I hope you won't be offended, but I'd like to suggest that we include Sandy in on this. She's been a real help in getting a lot of this information to us, and she's very analytical when it comes to thinking things through. When do you think we could see her?"

"Well, let me think a minute. The group is leaving the conference center sometime later today. I think maybe after dinner. Sometimes, when that's the case, Sandy just stays until they've gone. That way Eve doesn't have to come in at three o'clock for just a few hours of work. I'll call Sandy and make sure that's the case tonight."

CHAPTER SEVENTEEN

While Mitch showered, I called Sandy to see if she could meet us later at the Copper Kettle to discuss the case.

"Sure. I just don't know exactly what time I can get away," she said. "The doctors will all be down in the dining room between six and seven, and probably won't all leave until eight. A severe thunderstorm warning has been issued for our area for this evening, and some of the doctors are concerned that their flights may be affected. I've spent the last few hours trying to get some of them earlier flights, but I haven't had much success. So, at this point, I can't say what time I'll be getting out of here myself."

"Well, let me know when you know something. I can page Mitch later and tell him," I said.

"Alice came to see me again. Something else has come up. You'll probably want to let Mitch know right away. Alice told me she found the missing contact lens. She said that late yesterday she was told that she should go to the doctor's room and give it a thorough cleaning. She was told that it wasn't considered a crime scene anymore. While she was cleaning, she found a contact lens stuck to the edge of the carpet near the window. She says she knew right away what it was because her brother wears them."

"Now how did everyone miss it before?" I asked.

"You tell me," Sandy answered. "Of course, Alice was too afraid to call the sheriff, and so she came to me and begged me to tell Mitch about it. I told her he'd need her to show him exactly where the contact lens is, but she said 'Oh, he won't need me. I marked right where it is. I put a clean bathroom glass upside down over it. It's all protected.' She's too much, isn't she?"

"You can say that again," I said.

"Should I tell Ted about this?" Sandy asked. "He's not here right now. He's always got his Rotary Club luncheon on Friday."

I thought about that for a moment. "No. Let me tell Mitch first, and see what he says. I'll call you back," I said.

"Can you reach him?" Sandy asked.

"Yes, if I put my arm out about three feet," I said, laughing. "He's right next to me. Let me bring him up to date, and I'll call you right back."

I told Mitch about Alice's latest evidence. He sat on the sofa in his thinking pose. "I should go over there now and talk to Alice," he said wearily.

"Oh, she's long gone," I said. "She's scared to death of all you guys. Finding the lens in the room makes it look like there may have been a struggle there and then he was taken down to the pool and drowned, doesn't it?"

"Yes, it's beginning to look that way," Mitch said.

"Should Sandy tell Ted about the contact lens?" I asked.

"No, I'll handle that," he said.

"What's your plan?" I asked, sitting next to him.

"When I get to the conference center, I'm going to photograph the lens in the doctor's room. Deputy Don will be a witness, and we can always subpoena Alice later if necessary," Mitch said. "Here's what I want you to have Sandy do. After Don and I have left, have Sandy tell Ted that Alice just found the missing contact lens in the doctor's room. And tell Ted she hasn't had a chance to call the sheriff about it. I'm willing to bet that Ted will call his buddy, Lyndon, to come help him look for the lens. But I wouldn't be a bit surprised if they come back empty-handed, if you follow me."

"Do you mean that you think they're going to dispose of the evidence?" I asked.

"That's what I'm thinking," he said. "This may

be just what we've been waiting for. If they do tamper with the evidence, we'll know for sure that both of them are mixed up in this mess somehow. The way it stands right now, the sheriff is getting ready to call off the investigation. He says he just doesn't have enough evidence to accuse anyone of murder."

"How could it be that everyone who had searched that room before this has missed that contact lens?" I asked. "That seems very unlikely, doesn't it?"

"No, I don't think so," Mitch answered. "It's such a small thing. And maybe it was just because Alice was in there at a particular time of day, and the light just hit it a certain way that it was just now noticed."

"I guess that's possible," I said.

"Call Sandy and tell her I'm on my way. Tell her about the plan, but she's not to talk to Ted until after I've left the scene, okay?" Mitch said.

"Okay," I said, reaching for the phone. "Oh, and Sandy said she'll have to let us know when she can meet us at the Copper Kettle tonight. She's not sure at this point what time all the doctors will be leaving. Seems there's a severe thunderstorm warning, and there's a chance some of the flights might be affected. I told her we're going to try to come up with our own theory about how and why Dr. Henderson was murdered. Hopefully, we'll get a different answer than the one the sheriff has come up with."

"Sounds good. Look, I've got to get going. I'll call Don from the car," Mitch said.

We kissed good-bye in the doorway, and I climbed into bed. I thought about Mitch and Don leaving the conference center in a little while. What if Ted was coming back from his luncheon and passed two patrol cars leaving the Center. Would he know something was up? At a time like this, it didn't seem advantageous to have only one road in to or out of the property. It wound through heavily wooded areas and expanses of open fields, but there was only the one road.

This was always an appealing feature for security purposes when the conference center hosted high-level government meetings, especially when the President or other world leaders were in attendance. The Secret Service could easily cover the only road to the property. Employees' cars were searched at this point, and the media were turned away.

At other locations on the property, sharpshooters were stationed. Air traffic was forbidden in the air space over the entire 200 acre parcel, and the agents deemed the grounds to be secure. At times like those, I always felt like I was in the safest place on earth. I didn't feel that way now.

CHAPTER EIGHTEEN

I was dreaming about hearing gunfire over and over and not knowing where Mitch was or whether or not he was safe. I could hear his voice, but I was seeing my father's face. I woke with a start at the next loud boom of thunder.

Gunther was under the covers so close to me that I could feel him trembling. "It's okay, you coward," I said. "I know how you feel."

The clock showed that it was nearly 5:30, but it seemed much darker outside. I peeked through the blind and was met by a huge jag of lightning.

I called Sandy. She didn't answer until the seventh ring. "Are you okay?" I asked.

"Yes, I guess so. We're having a bad storm here, and the lights keep going out for a few seconds at a time. I'm afraid we're going to lose the phone."

"What happened earlier?" I asked. "What happened with Ted and the evidence?"

"I did just what Mitch said to do. I waited until I saw Mitch and Don drive away, then I told Ted that Alice had just found the missing contact lens, and how she had left it for safekeeping. I added that this was what Mitch said the sheriff had been looking for. I told Ted I hadn't had a chance to call the sheriff. He offered to do it, and ended up meeting Sheriff Clark over there a little while later. He asked me where Alice was—he wanted to talk to her. I said I was sure she had gone for the day."

"Good job, Sandy," I said.

"I hope so," she said.

"Where is Ted now?" I asked.

"He left a little after five—didn't even say good night," Sandy said.

"What a jerk. Well, his turn's coming," I said. "Sandy, do you know yet when you can meet Mitch and me?" I asked.

"Not exactly. The group should be coming back from the dining room anytime now. They kept me pretty busy this afternoon confirming some airline reservations for tonight. I still have a few calls to make before they get back here. I had to verify that the airport shuttle bus from BWI would be arriving at 7:30 to transport those who hadn't driven their own cars.

"It was after 3:30 when I saw Sheriff Clark's car pull away from the parking lot behind the guest building. Ted came out to the desk a few moments later, and said that I must have misunderstood. He said that Alice didn't find anything in the doctor's room. She thought that she had, but she was mistaken. He said we got the sheriff out here for nothing."

"That's great!" I said. "This is what Mitch thought would happen. This proves that the sheriff and Ted are both involved in Dr. Henderson's murder."

"Do you think they know that we're on to them?" Sandy asked, her voice softer.

"I don't know why they should," I said. "Look, the lights are flickering here. I'm going to grab a quick shower before I lose the power. I'll talk to you soon."

The thunder was loud enough to be heard over the running water, but I could hear the phone ringing as soon as I shut it off. Grabbing a towel, I took four giant steps into my bedroom and answered. I tried to dry off while Mitch brought me up to date. The occasional loud crack of thunder only added to my nervousness. Gunther had now taken refuge under the bed, just the tip of his tail sticking out.

Mitch told me how Alice had placed a glass over the lens she found in Dr. Henderson's room, and that he and Don had photographed it as evidence. I told Ted what Sandy had told me about Ted's reaction and how he'd told her it had all been a misunderstanding.

After leaving the conference center and before going home, Mitch said he had gone to the sheriff's office hoping to get the sheriff to tell him about finding or not finding the lens. The sheriff said that this whole case had been just a bunch of empty leads from the start. He was sick and tired of stupid people interfering with everything. He told Mitch that he had just been called to the conference center on another wild goose chase. A housekeeper had said that she had found the missing contact lens in Dr. Henderson's room, but when he and Ted had gone to retrieve it, there was nothing there.

"I have to tell you that by that time I was feeling pretty certain of the sheriff's guilt in the murder. I asked him if Ted had ever been asked to provide an alibi for Monday night," Mitch said.

"You didn't!" I said. "What did he do?" Mitch said that the sheriff became belligerent, reminding Mitch that he was not in charge of this case and that he had better watch his step. "So, what else has to happen to convince you that both your boss and my boss are criminals?" I said impatiently.

"It sure looks that way, doesn't it?" Mitch

asked. "I'm anxious for you and Sandy and me to put our heads together tonight and try to figure this thing out. She's going to be at the conference center until about eight, you said?"

"It looks that way," I answered. "But she's really not sure. I'll call her back soon."

"Damn!" Mitch said.

"What's wrong?" I asked.

"My pager's going off. It's the sheriff. I'll call you right back."

I finished drying myself and had my underwear on when Mitch called back. "Sheriff Clark is sending me out on a Good Samaritan run. A big storm just slammed through the western edge of the county. It will probably hit here anytime. He says there are some folks out there who think a tornado might have passed through their trailer park. Did some damage. Might be some injuries. They're pretty shaken up and he wants me to go and check on them."

"Trailer park?" I said. "The one all the way out on Burton Road? That's where Ellen lives."

"Well, it may just be a coincidence. Anyway, I'd better get out there," Mitch said.

"Mitch," I said.

"Yes?"

"Please be very careful," I said, my throat dry.

"Don't worry," he said. "I'll meet you and Sandy at the center as soon as I can." He hung up without saying good-bye.

The wind had kicked up and rain was beginning to hit the windows pretty hard. I finished dressing as the lights flickered a few times. "Sorry I have to leave you, Gunther. You'll be okay. Just stay where you are. I'm sure the storm won't be able to find you under the bed, you big chicken," I said.

I picked up my wallet and keys and turned off the bedroom light. A few seconds later, I retraced my steps and clicked the light on again. I opened the bottom drawer of my nightstand and took out my pistol. I loaded it and tucked it into the rear waistband of my jeans. I stopped at the hall closet to pull on my rain slicker and grab a baseball cap before going out into the storm.

Chapter Nineteen

I got to the conference center a little before seven, parking as close as I could. I ran through the downpour and struggled to pull the heavy glass door open against the wind. The gusts were fierce, rattling the windows and doors, and the thunder made it sound like the storm was right on top of the building.

"Hey, what's up?" I asked Sandy, as I brushed water from my coat. I took off the baseball cap and shook it out, fluffing my hair with my fingers. "Everybody down at dinner?"

"No, they're finished dinner," she said. "Those who had their cars here have already left. The rest are over at the guest building, getting their suitcases and things. Now we just need the airport shuttle to get here and get everybody else out before this storm gets any worse. Where's Mitch?"

"He'll be here as soon as he can. The sheriff sent him out to check on a possible tornado. It was spotted in the same trailer park where Ellen lives," I said

"I never heard what happened when you went out there to talk to her. What did Ellen say?" Sandy asked.

"Not much. She was gone," I said. "I talked to an old lady who lives across the street and she said that Ellen's been missing since yesterday—right after the sheriff talked to her."

"Oh, no. Poor Ellen. What could possibly have happened to her?" Sandy asked.

"Beats the hell out of me," I said. "Her car was still there and she left wash on the line, so it sure looks like she left in a big hurry. I have no way of finding out where she's gone or why. Maybe you could call your buddy, Alice, and see if she's got any ideas."

"What does Mitch think is going on?" Sandy asked.

"He's still having a hard time believing his boss is crooked. But I think the episode this afternoon with the sheriff and Ted tampering with evidence may have finally convinced Mitch that it's true. We need to try to see if we can figure out how Dr. Henderson was killed. We've only got a few pieces of evidence, but we've got to start somewhere," I said just barely above the thunder. "It looks like this case is cooling off, and there may be a good chance that the sheriff is going to pull the plug on the investigation soon."

"I'm not even going to bother with straightening the conference room tonight," Sandy said. "I'll have time to do it Monday morning. The National Security Agency will be here next week, you know."

"Oh, that's right. Our old NSA buddies. Seems like they were just here. Oh, well, I always like it when they come to see us. I feel protected. Any of the big leaders going to be here?" Jill asked.

"I don't know yet," Sandy said. "I honestly haven't had time to check the list of attendees. There will be time for that on Monday. Oh, have you heard any talk about the Secretary of State having a meeting here next month? Maureen said she heard something about it. And you know how good the kitchen grapevine is. I know the White House usually doesn't give us very much notice, but they're really cutting it pretty close. I'll ask Claire on Monday. She'll know," Sandy said. Then suddenly, "Oh, that's right, you wanted me to call Alice," she said, reaching for the Rolodex.

"Claire's still here," I said. "Her car's outside."

As if on cue, I heard Claire's heels clicking on the stairs behind me. "I guess it's not going to let up anytime soon, is it?" she asked.

"Doesn't look like it," I said.

"You two better leave as soon as you can," Claire

said. "I just talked to my neighbor, and she said that the storm's already washed out some roads and knocked down a few trees in my neighborhood. If that happens on our road out here, you'll be stranded back here with no way in or out. You are leaving soon, I hope?"

I didn't want her to know that Mitch was meeting us. "As soon as possible," I lied.

"I thought it would be okay to wait and clean up the conference room on Monday morning. I don't think it will matter to anyone, do you?" Sandy asked Claire.

"Not in the least," she answered. "You two get out of here, okay?" she said, opening her umbrella at the door. We watched her hurry off into the near-darkness, trying to hold onto her umbrella in the high winds, avoid puddles, and carry her bulging briefcase.

I paced at the front door, glancing out at the violent night, while Sandy dialed Alice's number. "No one's home," she declared, hanging up.

"Just for fun, try Ellen's number, will you?" I said, handing her the folded piece of paper from the pocket of my jeans.

After a moment she said, "No one's there either," the receiver still at her ear.

I stopped my pacing and turned to face her. "Look, here's the way I see it," I said, leaning on the desk. "Ted and Mrs. H. first met each other about a year and a half ago, or whenever it was that she was here for her meeting. She overheard the housekeepers sharing some gossip, and she got her panties all twisted, and complained to Ted, who found out that it was Ellen who had the big mouth, and fired her."

"I remember what it was that Alice said she thought the gossip was about," Sandy said. "Ellen was saying that two people slept in Mrs. Henderson's room."

We were silent for a moment, before I slowly said, "My, my, my. That certainly is interesting. Do you think it was Ted?"

"Not likely, if they had just met each other. That was Mrs. Henderson's first and only conference here. Of course, maybe they knew each other before that," she said. "How could we ever find out?"

"I don't know. And I hate to admit it, but Ted's probably not stupid enough to do something like bunk in with Mrs. H. right here under the noses of all his employees. And besides, he wasn't separated from his wife yet. Not that that really means anything," I said. "But maybe the gossip wasn't just gossip. Maybe Mrs. H. did have somebody else in her bed. Could been somebody else attending the conference with her, or it could have been somebody who just showed up at night. Either way, maybe it gave Ted ideas about this lady," I suggested.

I continued trying to put some more pieces together. "Suppose Dr. H. found out about the affair his wife was having with Ted? That wouldn't get *him* killed, would it? Suppose Ted confronted the doctor about giving Mrs. H. a divorce? Mitch said that the Philly police said that their marriage was definitely on the rocks, and according to her, he wouldn't let her end it. Suppose Mrs. H. decided to end it her way, and did him in herself? Do you think a woman could drown a man?" I said.

"Possibly if he was drunk or drugged," Sandy said thoughtfully. "Do you know if the coroner found any evidence of either of those things? But, don't forget that the coroner did say he had what appeared to be a bump on his head. He said it could have happened when the doctor jumped into the pool. What if Mrs. Henderson hit him, or if *Ted* hit him? If the doctor was completely out or even just dazed, they both could have easily overpowered him and drowned him in the pool."

"Well, yes, but back up a minute," I said. "It looks like they may have all been in the doctor's room first, because that's where Alice found the missing contact lens. It's likely that someone hit the doctor on the head there and that's how he lost the lens. Then they must have decided to go ahead and get rid of him. Maybe they had already planned to drown him. Or maybe they just thought it up on the spot. In any case, they would have to change his clothes—putting on his swim trunks, and then somehow carrying him down to the pool without being seen."

"Yes, and since Ted had you busy sitting at a desk doing all those checklists, he would have known that there would have been very little chance of you witnessing all this," Sandy said.

"Well, actually, I got here a little after the fact," I said. "But that was our leader's suggestion. He told me to come in later to do that project. Boy, this is looking more and more like premeditated murder to me."

"So, we've got Ted and Mrs. Henderson somehow getting her husband's body into the pool without being seen. The doctor's lost one of his lenses, and in all the confusion, they don't even think about removing the other one so that it would look like he had really gone for a morning swim. They must not have considered that the coroner might be able to put the time of death much earlier than that," she said.

"Well, it usually is a little detail like that that hangs most folks," I said with a grin.

"I guess so," Sandy said. "Okay, so now one or both of them has drowned the doctor. What do they do next? The other pieces of evidence that we have from Alice are the dried towels, the unused soap, and the wet carpet in the elevator."

"Well, it would seem to me that somebody got pretty wet holding the doctor down in the pool, and maybe he even struggled with them, so maybe Ted and his lady went back up to the doctor's room to make sure they hadn't left any loose ends. Whoever's wet drips all over the carpet in the elevator, figuring it'll be dry by the morning, or maybe not even noticing it. But with the elevator not being used during the night and little or no air circulation inside, the rug stayed wet. They use the towels in the bathroom to dry off. The towels didn't get wet from anybody showering or taking a bath, just like Alice said. They just used them to dry off," I said, folding my arms across my chest, feeling quite satisfied with this scenario.

"I guess that all makes sense," Sandy said. "And don't forget that Alice also said she had the feeling someone tried to make it look like the bed had been slept in. At least they thought to do that, so that it would look like he'd gone out for a swim after waking up in the morning. So, where do we go from here?" she asked.

"I don't know. Mrs. H. has gone back to Philly to bury her husband. Ted's never been questioned enough to see if he can come up with any good answers, and we don't even know if he's got an alibi. But she does," I said. "That bothers me."

"Did Mitch say what else he could do to keep the investigation going?" she asked.

"Not really," I said. "The sheriff chewed him out but good this afternoon when Mitch asked if Ted had an alibi. The sheriff told Mitch he wasn't running this investigation. So Mitch feels his hands are tied. He just doesn't know where to go from here," I said. "Somehow I keep thinking that finding Ellen would help us learn a lot. But at this point, we don't know where in the hell she is."

We were both silent for a moment, my frustration growing. Then Sandy said, "Maybe we should just forget about all of this, Jill. What if we're wrong?"

I took several seconds to study Sandy's face before answering her question with one of my own. "What if we're right?"

Deep into our discussion, we had forgotten all about the airport shuttle bus, which arrived promptly at 7:30. The driver pulled up in front of the conference center, and gave the horn two long blasts. Neither of us had any notion of running out to greet him, so he finally sprang from the bus and ran for the front door, jumping over the puddles.

"Where is everybody?" he asked. "We'd better get going. The wind is so strong, I wouldn't be surprised if one of these millions of trees you got back here don't blow over and block the road. There's no other way outta here, is there?"

"No, there sure isn't," Sandy said, slowly shaking her head.

"There's already a car down in a ditch," he said. "Only about a quarter mile away. Has anybody walked back here for help? Wasn't anybody still in the car, as far as I could tell. And I sure didn't pass anybody walking. I definitely woulda stopped."

"What kind of car?" Sandy asked apprehensively.

"Old station wagon. White with the driver's door painted in primer," he said.

"That's Alice's car," Sandy gasped. I walked to the door, peering out into the violent night.

"Maybe you'd better call the cops or somebody, if you think she might be still out there somewhere. It's really a bad one. I heard on the radio there's an unconfirmed report of a tornado around here," he said.

"Well, there's nowhere else she'd go in this storm," I said. "She'd have to come back here, unless somebody picked her up."

"I guess it's possible that one of the doctors who left a little while ago could have seen Alice and picked her up. But where would they go? They would have definitely come back here, don't you think? All the kitchen employees must still be here, too. They're usually here at least two hours after dinner," Sandy said.

"I wish Mitch were here," I said, pacing again. "There's too many loose ends, and more are unraveling every minute. A few minutes ago, I was worried about finding Ellen. Now we may have lost Alice, too."

"If you wouldn't mind, could you drive over to the three-story building at the end of this road?" Sandy said to the driver. "That's where all your passengers are." After the driver left, Sandy turned to me, "What should we do about Alice and her car? Shouldn't we call somebody?"

"We could try Mitch, but he's out at the trailer park, and he's probably got his hands full. Hopefully, he'll be on his way here soon, but he wouldn't recognize Alice's car. Maybe we should call him and give him a heads-up," I said. I used Sandy's phone to dial Mitch's pager number, then left the number for the front desk. The thunder seemed to have eased up a bit, or maybe I was just getting used to it. The lights flickered again.

"I've got an idea," Sandy said. She dialed the Reservations Desk and asked whoever answered if they remembered seeing Alice leave earlier. I saw the look of concern deepen on Sandy's face. "No? That's what I was afraid of. Her car's been spotted in a ditch not far from the conference center. We don't know where she is now. I'll keep trying her at home," she said. Then she alternated trying Ellen's number and Alice's, and finally gave up.

"Well, I can't think of anybody else we should call to help find Alice. I'm going to go out to where that guy said her car is, and have a look around," I said.

"Oh, I wish you wouldn't. The weather's just too bad, Jill. Please, don't," Sandy begged.

"But what if Alice is out there and hurt? Look, I've got to do something. When Mitch calls, tell him what's going on," I said, turning toward the front door. I snapped the front of my slicker securely, and holding the baseball cap on my head with one hand, pushed my way out the door with the other.

CHAPTER TWENTY

My wipers couldn't keep the rain off my windshield, and my headlights barely cut through the gloom. I backtracked from the conference center down the road exactly a quarter of a mile. Nothing. I crept along, checking both sides of the road for Alice's car. The bus driver must have been wrong about the distance. I drove another half mile and, seeing no car, doubled back, still peering into the semidarkness.

As I passed a narrow dirt lane on my left, I caught a glimpse of something large and light-colored. I hit the brakes so fast that the truck went into a skid, hydroplaning for maybe twenty yards. I was able to stop it just a few feet from a pretty steep ravine and turned the truck around. I pulled onto the dirt road, driving slowly, and tried to judge the depth of the mud. I wasn't anxious to get stuck out there, so I stopped, switched off the engine and hopped out. My boots sank down a few inches into the muck. I reached back under the seat, grabbed a flashlight, and switched it on. As I straightened back up, I felt the reassuring cold metal of my gun, still in my waistband.

With the wind driving the rain against my back, I was able to see a white station wagon pulled at an awkward angle just off the overgrown path. These so-called roads were once used as fire trails. If there were ever a forest fire on any of this acreage, fire engines wouldn't have any way to get back into the woods to fight it. Several years ago, trails like this one had been cleared just for that purpose. But the need to use them never came up, and no one made any attempt to keep them open, and the trees had pretty much reclaimed these areas. The limbs jutted out into the path and the top branches formed a solid canopy overhead.

As I approached the car, I could see that the right front wheel was sunk deep in the mud. Every step I took led me deeper and deeper into the tunnel of trees. I stopped to listen to see if I could hear the engine running, but it was raining too hard to tell. I could hear the rapid pinging of the hard rain hitting the roof and hood. The interior of the car was completely dark, making it impossible to see from where I was if anyone was inside. I looked behind me and to either side before continuing. When I was close enough to the car to touch the rear bumper, I heard a noise. I stopped and cocked my head to hear better. "Alice?" I called. Again a noise, but the wind made it hard to tell which direction it was coming from.

Then I caught movement out of the corner of my eye. A face suddenly appeared at the rectangle of glass over the tailgate of the station wagon. I must have jumped three feet in the air. I didn't drop the flashlight, but I was shaking so much that I had to hold on to it with both hands.

A woman's face was squinting at me through the glass, both hands trying to shield her eyes from the glare of my flashlight. "Alice?" I yelled. "Alice? It's me. It's Jill." I swung the flashlight around so that it was shining on my face. I wasn't sure she'd recognize me in the state she was in.

She dropped her hands down from her face and slowly nodded her head. I watched as she awkwardly crawled out from under a torn blanket and climbed over the rear seat. I tried the handle, but the door was locked. She opened the door from the inside, stepped out, and hunched her shoulders as the rain hit her full force in the face.

"What happened, for God's sake? What are you doing out here?" I asked.

"Hiding," she said simply.

"What in the hell from? The airport bus driver said he saw your car in a ditch alongside the road. How'd you get way back here?" I asked.

"Can we just get out of here? Please? Ted may come back looking for me," she said, as she started making her way through the mud.

"Ted? What's Ted got to do with this?" I asked. Alice was walking more quickly now toward my truck, and I caught up with her, both of us yanking the doors open at the same time. We slammed the doors against the driving rain and I started the engine.

"Lock the doors," she said quickly. She had brought the blanket with her and even though it was drenched, held it tightly around her shoulders.

"Alice," I said patiently. "You've got to tell me what's going on. I'm not leaving here until you do."

Her huge eyes peered at me from behind the wet glasses. She wiped the lenses with the back of her hand, and shivered. I started the engine and turned the heater on low. Nervously, she looked out all the windows before beginning her story.

"Do you know what happened this afternoon? About that missing contact lens that I found?" I nodded. "Well, it was there. I swear to God it was there, Jill. I told Sandy and Sandy was supposed to tell Mitch. I saw Mitch and another deputy go in Dr. Henderson's room a little later. I figured, good, they found it and I didn't have to get involved, and that was that." She was still shivering, and I turned the heater up a notch.

"Well, I got real busy with vacuuming the dining room, see, and I didn't get finished until after four. So I was late leaving. You know how they get about overtime. But I just had to finish, you know? We've been short-handed the last two days. Sue's on vacation, you know. Anyway, I go out to my car and Ted's standing out in the parking lot. Not right near my car, but out toward the end. It wasn't raining so bad just then. Well, I didn't think anything about it, and just as I was getting in my car, he comes hurrying up to me and asks me what do I think I'm doing, making up stories about evidence. Jill, what reason could I have for doing something like that? Anyway, Ted's really mad at me and starts yelling, and I started crying, and he tells me that there was no evidence, and there is no more case, and the police are really fed up with all my stories, and I'd better just stop it."

I turned the heater off and asked, "Did he threaten you any more than that?"

"He said that it was my word against everyone else's, and that if I didn't stop making up stories, something might happen," Alice said, still shivering.

"Did he say what might happen? Did he say anything else, Alice?" I asked impatiently.

"No," Alice said. "He walked away. He was still really mad. I was shaking so bad, I didn't think I could drive. I just sat there for the longest while. I didn't know if I should talk to somebody about what happened. I wanted to talk to Sandy, but I was afraid to go back into the conference building. I figured Ted might be in there. So I just sat there a good long while. I swear, Jill, everything I've said is true. Honest," Alice said, her voice shaking.

"I finally felt okay to drive and got a little ways down the road, out of sight of the center and all, and a car came up behind me real fast. I thought it was going to pass me, but we were coming up on a pretty bad curve. Anyhow, it was really close to me, but I couldn't see who was driving. But I know it was a man. It just kept right behind me, real close. The wind had started to blow real hard, and it was starting to rain real hard again, too. I thought I'd just better get out of his way, so I pulled off the road. Then the other car went racing on down the road. But I must have pulled over too far, because my tire got stuck in the mud. Then I got upset again, cause I didn't know what to do. I looked up and saw that same car coming back down the road toward me again. I was so scared, I ran into the woods. He probably saw me run, but I guess he didn't stop. I stayed hiding in there for a long time, hoping the rain would let up a little, but it never did."

"Was it Ted's car? Do you think Ted was the

driver?" I asked.

Alice blinked back at me, her eyes searching my face. "Maybe," she answered. "Anyway, I figured he must have gone, and so I got back in my car. It took me quite a while to get my car out of the mud, but, thank God, I did. By then, it was raining so hard and the wind was so bad, I was afraid to drive any further, I couldn't even see the road, and I was afraid that the same car might come back looking for me, so I pulled off onto this dirt road. I guess that was pretty stupid, because I got stuck again."

I was exhausted from Alice's story, and forced myself to take a few breaths to clear my head. I put the truck into reverse and carefully backed down the muddy path. "Do you know where Ellen is?" I asked.

"No," Alice said anxiously. "I've been trying to call her all day."

I felt the back tires hit the paved surface of the main road. I put the truck into first gear, and said, "Let's get the hell out of here. I'm taking you back to the conference center. We're going to get to the bottom on this."

We rode in silence until we were within sight of the conference center. The guest facility and kitchen were completely dark. For a second I figured the power had gone off, but then saw that there were a few lights coming from the conference center's windows. All the staff in the other buildings had gone. Sandy must be the only one left. She was waiting for Mitch and me.

As I passed the employee lot next to the conference building, Alice said, "That's the car! I'm pretty sure that's the car that tried to run me off the road. Is it Ted's?" I looked to where she was pointing and saw Ted's large dark sedan parked at the end of the employee lot. The only other car on the lot was Sandy's.

"Yes," I said, suddenly feeling alarmed. I pulled the truck as close to the front door as I could, and reached for the driver's door handle. Alice gripped my arm. "Can I just wait here? Please?" she asked.

"No way. I'm keeping my eye on you. You're coming inside for safekeeping. Now!" I barked. Alice quickly opened her door, and we both ran through the rain toward the building. I grabbed the door handle and pulled, but was startled to find the door locked. While the rain continued to beat down on us, I unlocked the door with the set of master keys I had in my coat pocket.

We stood just inside the door, brushing water from our coats, when Alice whispered, "Where's Sandy?" I looked up and was surprised that Sandy wasn't sitting at the desk. "Her car's still out there," whispered Alice.

"For crying out loud," I said. "I find one of you and the other one gets lost! Well, she couldn't have gone very far."

Chapter Twenty-one

The lights had been turned off in the kitchen and most of the ones in the lobby, too. The desk stood in shadow. I crossed the lobby and searched the top of the desk, looking to see if Sandy had left any kind of note, but she hadn't. Alice stood about ten inches inside the door, still clutching her soaked plaid blanket.

I sat heavily in the chair, and said, "I'm going to page Mitch and Don. We need to get the cavalry here," I said, and was punching in his number, when I heard Ted's voice behind me.

"Hang up," he said softly.

I turned to see him standing in the doorway of the darkened kitchen.

"Ted?" I said. "What are you doing here at this hour?" I asked, smiling and trying to sound casual.

"You girls sure have vivid imaginations," he said, emerging from the shadows and shaking his head.

He walked quickly from the kitchen and headed

toward the front door. With a cry of alarm, Alice scurried out of his way. Ted peered out into the darkness, then turned to face me. I rose from my seat and began walking toward Ted, not liking the way this was going.

He held up his left hand like a traffic cop, and reached into his coat pocket with his right. "You're not going anywhere. Might as well make yourselves comfortable, girls" he said, as he withdrew a small pistol from his pocket. Alice gasped and backed away until she was touching the lobby wall. I took one, maybe two steps toward Ted, before he said, "Don't do it, Jill. Don't do it." I stopped, remembering that I didn't know where Sandy was or what condition she might be in.

"Let's go into the conference room and join your other friend," he said, waving the pistol with a jerking motion.

I had to pry Alice away from the wall, and push her in the right direction since her legs weren't working very well. Mine were doing only a little better.

Just the back corner of the conference room was lit by a single row of overhead lights. I saw Sandy sitting in one of the plush chairs, watching us. Her eyes were red. The incessant rain drummed on the low roof, but a soft rumble of now distant thunder told me that maybe the storm would be letting up soon.

"Sit," Ted commanded. Alice immediately took a seat in the chair next to Sandy's. I walked closer to Sandy and Alice, but continued standing.

Ted's eyes darted nervously. He looked first to the large bank of windows now covered by the blinds, then through the open conference room door, toward the lobby. He cocked his head every few minutes, probably listening for approaching vehicles. Who was he expecting? He began pacing from the windows to the door, anxiously rubbing the back of his neck. Suddenly, he stopped pacing, and turned to face us.

"Tell them, Sandy," he said.

Sandy looked at me, then Alice, then back to me. "Ted heard everything, Jill. He was in the building when you and I were talking about the murder. He heard us figure how out it was done." Alice gasped and huddled forward in her chair, staring at the floor.

"You know, that story you girls made up wasn't that bad," Ted said. "I mean I can see where you might have thought that something like that could have really happened. But you forgot one very important thing. Sheriff Clark doesn't agree with you. He doesn't believe that anyone is guilty of drowning Dr. Henderson. It was just a very unfortunate accident. The sheriff doesn't believe all those stories that Alice made up, either. At first, I thought I just needed to make the three of you realize that this is all so ridiculous, and that you should forget about it. But now I don't think that is going to work, do you?" he asked, the pistol looking larger in his hand.

I was considering a response when he suddenly said loudly, "Sit down, Jill, you've got to listen to me! I'll tell you what really happened."

"Ted, don't be foolish," I said firmly. "Sure, I'll sit down and listen. We'll all sit here and listen to your version of what happened. Just don't get upset, okay? And put that gun away, for Pete's sake. There's no need for that." I sat in a chair against the wall, about twenty feet away from Sandy and Alice. "Okay, Ted, we're a captive audience. Were ready to hear what you've got to say," I said.

Ted suddenly looked at the gun in his hand as if it were the first time he'd noticed it. He gently placed it on the edge of the conference table next to where he was standing. "Okay, you're right. I don't need that, do I? We're just going to talk. That's all."

He turned away from us and slowly walked to the windows, peering through the blinds into the blackness. He turned to face us before speaking.

"Look, this whole business of Dr. Henderson's death has been blown all out of proportion. The man drowned in the pool while going for an early morning swim. That's all there is to it. How it ever got turned into a murder, I don't know," he said.

"The coroner's report would probably refresh your memory," I said firmly. Ted's lies were beginning to annoy me, and I decided I had to challenge him. I turned to look at Sandy, who was staring, mouth open in disbelief at my callousness. Alice was staring, too, her eyes wide. "It was no accidental drowning, and you know it," I continued. "And so does Sheriff Clark."

Ted shook his head, before responding. "Jill, the sheriff doesn't agree. There isn't any evidence to prove that what happened to the doctor was anything more than an accident. There is no murder. There is no case. Don't you all understand that? I know Alice does," Ted said, nodding in her direction.

"Because you threatened her," I said. "She told me that you tried to run her car off the road. And that was after you had already threatened her this afternoon in the parking lot."

I didn't know if we could walk away from this situation without anyone getting hurt, but that's what I began praying for.

We all heard it at the same time—an

approaching car. Thank God, Mitch was finally here!

"Here's the sheriff now," Ted said. "Maybe he'll have a better chance of convincing you that there was no murder."

Sandy and I made eye contact, and she raised her eyebrows in question, but I just winked at her. I was certain that it had to be Mitch outside, and not the sheriff, as Ted thought.

We all listened to the sound of the front door opening, briefly letting in the noise of the wind. The door closed again, abruptly cutting off the outside sounds. Ted picked up the gun and walked through the doorway into the lobby. I heard his voice in a low murmur and he immediately reentered the room, followed by Sheriff Clark. My heart sank as I realized that not only wasn't it Mitch, but that he might not get here in time to save us from ourselves. Where could he be? What had happened to him?

I wasn't sure how this scene would play out, but I knew we three girls were no match for the two armed men we now faced. I was immediately angry with myself for not trying to use my gun on Ted before the sheriff got here. But I knew I wouldn't have taken any chances with Sandy and Alice in the room as targets. Bolstered by his friend's presence, Ted once again set the pistol down on the conference table.

"Evening, ladies," the sheriff said casually. "Seems like there are a few loose ends need tying up around here. Ted here tells me that you think you know how the good doctor was murdered. Why don't we start with you, Jill? What do you figure happened?"

Ted was looking at the sheriff with a puzzled look on his face. "Lyndon?" he asked. "What are you doing?"

"Just hold on a minute, Ted. Let's just give these little ladies a chance to show us how smart they are," the sheriff answered. "Jill?"

"Why should I? What does it matter now?" I asked. "You've got us all here. All your witnesses. What are you going to do with us? And whatever your answer is, don't you think that might look just a little bit suspicious?"

"There goes that imagination again," Ted said.

"Not so fast, Ted," the sheriff said. "I still want to hear it from them. How'd they figure out that you killed Dr. Henderson?" Again, Ted looked uneasily at the sheriff. "Jill?" the sheriff prompted.

I decided to buy us some more time. Mitch had to be here any minute! I sat up straight, squared my shoulders, and began listing all the evidence that had been presented to us by Alice.

I must have been making some sense, because I saw concerned looks crossing the faces of both the sheriff and Ted.

I talked about the wet rug in the elevator, the used towels and the unused bar of soap in the bathroom. I described the details of the coroner's report that had first aroused suspicion, and talked about the kiss that I had witnessed between Mrs. Henderson and Ted. I told about the conversation I'd had with Ellen's neighbor, and about finding Alice after Ted's confrontation with her.

"Good work," said the sheriff. "You're really very close to the truth. Ted, I think you should have a seat, too. I'll be right back." He briskly walked from the room and we could hear the front door open. Instead of taking a seat, Ted resumed his pacing. I turned to look at the others. Alice was slumped back in her chair, eyes closed. Sandy was carefully watching Ted.

The front door opened and closed again and the sheriff led Widow Henderson into the room. Ted spun around to face them. "Kate! What are you doing here?" he demanded.

"I don't know what you've been saying, Ted, but I've told the sheriff everything." She spoke softly, and I found myself straining to hear what she was saying. "I told him how you left Joanna for me. How you tried to talk to my husband about giving me a divorce so that we could be married. And how things got out of hand, and how the two of you fought, and in your anger, you hit Roger and then drowned him in the pool," she said without emotion. She took three strides with those long legs and sat in one of the plush chairs, crossing her legs, but not pulling her skirt down.

Ted's mouth gaped open, and his eyes bulged. "What are you talking about?" he said loudly. "That's not true! None of it! You and I had been seeing each other for over a year before I left Joanna. You were the one who asked me to talk to your husband about giving you a divorce. I never said anything about marrying you! You were the one who argued with him and hit him on the head. And then we panicked because it had all gotten out of hand. But it was you who came up with plan to put him in the pool to make it look like he had hit his head while swimming. I never intended to hurt him. I thought we were just trying to scare him. You did that. But you said somebody was coming, and I must have panicked. I held him under because I didn't want him to make any noise. I only agreed to talk to him about the divorce, that's all. I never really meant to hurt the man. But...but you meant for me to kill him all along, didn't you?" Ted stood with his arms extended, palms upward, pleading for understanding. "Sheriff?" Ted asked.

"Well, Ted," Sheriff Clark said slowly. "I'm afraid what we got here is what we call a difference of opinion. I asked Mrs. Henderson to come down here from Philadelphia tonight because I wanted her to fill in some of the blanks for me. At first she refused to come, but when I told her that her alibi had just come unraveled, all of a sudden she seemed more than willing to come talk to me. Seems the young man who said they were in a meeting together on the night her husband drowned, suddenly remembered that he really wasn't with her after all. He had been with Mrs. Henderson at other meetings before that, although he doesn't have anything to do with banking. Also seems that the idea that Mrs. Henderson could have been involved in her husband's death put the fear of God in him right quick." The sheriff looked at Mrs. Henderson, who sat, arms folded across her chest, glaring at Ted.

"You're such a fool," she said softly, slowly shaking her head. "When we first met here a long time ago, you knew that I was just interested in having some fun. I never led you to believe that it would be only with you. You even knew I had someone here with me then. I told you that I didn't love Roger and that I wanted a divorce. But not to marry you or any other man," she said with a wicked laugh. "Why would I want to do that? More of the same? Yes, Ted, I used you. But to your credit, you were the only man I knew who was willing to help me confront Roger. Nothing I could say or do to him would make him divorce me. God knows I gave him the grounds to do it plenty of times."

She recrossed her legs, shifting in her chair and now stared at the sheriff.

Taking advantage of the stunned silence in the room, I knew I had to move fast. Ted lunged for the gun only seconds before I did. But when I saw that I was going to be too late to grab it, I turned instead and dashed through the doorway and out into the lobby.

CHAPTER TWENTY-TWO

I bolted from the room and raced down the hallway toward the back door. Just as I was unlocking the deadbolt, I heard a gun go off. I froze. I was pretty sure the sound had come from the conference room, and I had a sick feeling in my stomach. I slowly reached under my raincoat and pulled my gun from my waistband. Holding it down against my right thigh, I listened to my heart hammer in my chest. It was anybody's guess who'd been shot, but I didn't think Ted would come after me immediately, since he had enough people to keep him busy in the conference room.

I couldn't be absolutely sure that Ted had been the one to pull the trigger. The sheriff could have gotten his gun out and fired first. In all the confusion, anybody could have been hit. I was putting my money on a gun still being in Ted's hand, though. He seemed desperate enough. I could picture Ted now holding four people hostage in the conference room.

I couldn't hear any voices from where I was standing, but I was sure of one thing. I was going to be of more help to those people where I was, than back in there with them. At least this way I could go and get some real help.

I tried to figure out what I'd just witnessed in there. I didn't know what to think about the sheriff after what just happened. How come he wasn't on Ted's side, like we'd thought? Could we have all been that wrong? But if it was all some sort of trick, then Ted and the merry widow and the good sheriff were all in this together. But then why would the sheriff have gone to so much trouble to pull all the details out of the widow and me, building a case against Ted?

I wished Mitch would get here, so the sides would be more even. I didn't think I could count on Sandy for much help; she seemed too scared to react very quickly. And forget Alice. I just hoped she'd be smart enough to get out of the way if things got even more interesting. No one knew I was armed; the element of that surprise could help me even up the sides later.

I knew when Mitch did get here he'd take a reading on the cars and figure out that the sheriff and Ted were ganging up on us girls. But he wouldn't know about the grieving widow being here or the sheriff's strange behavior. I knew I had to warn Mitch and also let him know that I was no longer a guest of honor in the conference room, but on the outside, ready and more than willing to help him round up the bad guys.

I quietly opened the back door, stepped outside, and then quickly pushed it shut behind me. Although I braced myself for the downpour, the rain had almost stopped. There was just enough light coming from the building's windows for me to see to scurry away to the edge of the nearby woods. I circled the long way around, until I got back to my truck, opened the driver's door and quickly got in. The overhead light was on for only a few seconds. I returned the gun to my waistband, locked both doors and started the engine. I didn't care if Ted and the sheriff heard me leaving. They'd think I was going for help. Which I was. I was afraid, though, that Sandy would think I was abandoning them. She had to know that I wouldn't do that. She had to know that the only way I could help them was to come back with Mitch.

As I drove with one hand, I grabbed my phone and punched in the number for Mitch's pager. I left my number, then cleared the phone and waited for him to call back. Just before I got to the road where Alice's car had been abandoned, the phone rang. I hit the brakes, stopping the truck in the middle of the road. "Mitch?" I yelled into the phone.

"No, Jill. It's Don. Mitch gave me his pager in case you called. He's been trying to get to you. He said to tell you that everything's changed. He told me about you guys thinking that the sheriff was mixed up it the murder. He's not. It was all an act. It was his way of trying to trap Ted."

I was confused. How could this be? There had been so much evidence pointing to the sheriff being in on it, too. "I don't get it, Don," I said. "What about the second contact lens? We know that the sheriff disposed of it. How do you explain that?"

"The sheriff didn't get rid of it. Ted did. All by himself before the sheriff even got there. And while Mitch was out at the trailer park, he found Ellen. She's okay. The sheriff had come out to talk to her and it was the sheriff that suggested that she go away for a few days. He was afraid that Ted might get to her. She's been at her mother's," Don said.

I tried to sort all this out quickly. I still wasn't quite sure how to read what had gone on in the conference room just now. I told Don what the situation was. "Is Mitch on his way?" I asked eagerly.

"If he's not there by now, he's run into some trouble. We've had reports that there are several trees across the road leading back to the conference center. He may have had to turn back," Don said.

I felt my stomach tighten. I stared through the windshield, the wipers smearing the few remaining drops of rain that fell. I switched off the wipers. "Damn," I said.

"What are you going to do, Jill?" Don asked. "Can you wait until we can get the road cleared? I'll get the crews on it right away. Then we'll get some officers and an ambulance back there."

"I don't think it can wait that long, Don," I said. "When I last saw Ted, he looked pretty damned desperate. I already know what he's capable of. Now that I know the sheriff is one of the good guys, the situation is different. I feel certain they're all in danger. I've got to go back there."

"Jill, don't," Don said. "Ted's armed."

"So am I," I answered and hung up.

CHAPTER TWENTY-THREE

I made a U-turn and slowly headed back to the conference center. It had occurred to me that if I could pinpoint Mitch's location on our road, I could try to get close enough to him to pick him up. But Don had said that there were several trees down on this road and there was no telling how far apart we were from each other. It could be miles.

I tried to come up with a plan. I knew there was a good chance that someone in that room had been shot. They could even be dead or dying. I didn't know if the sheriff had been able to get his gun out before Ted grabbed his from the conference table. Hard to say who was running the show at this point. I was concerned what else Ted might do if cornered, and knew that I had no choice but to go back and try to be a hero. It occurred to me to have Don try to page the sheriff to find out what the situation was. But the information the sheriff gave Don might be at the point of Ted's gun. How would we know if he was lying? Ted might set up a trap. I had to assume that Ted was still holding everybody at gunpoint. He would believe that they were all his enemies. That they were all against him. And he would be right.

I parked my truck on the employee lot, and shut off the engine. I removed my raincoat and tossed it on the seat beside me. I made sure that the gun was secure in my waistband.

I sat in the dark, still trying to come up with a plan more original than waltzing into the room and asking Ted nicely to hand over the gun. It was then that I got the start of an idea. I wasn't really excited about it, but it was the only one I had. I decided I'd go with it until something better occurred to me. Hopefully it wouldn't get me or anybody else shot.

I started the engine and pulled the truck off the paved surface, heading toward the building. I kept the headlights off and slowly inched the truck over the grass toward the wall of windows that lined the conference room. About fifty feet from the building, I switched off the engine and allowed the truck to coast as far as it would go. It stopped about twenty feet from the windows and I prayed that Ted would not peer through the blinds for the next few minutes.

I pried the plastic cover off the overhead light

in the cab and pulled out the bulb. I opened the door, hidden by the darkness, but didn't close it.

I silently skirted the building, coming around to the front entrance, where the sheriff had parked his car, the engine still running and the headlights piercing the blackness. I eased the driver's door open and slid behind the steering wheel. The dashboard was ablaze with dials and lights, and from the radio speaker came broken phrases of chatter. I studied the controls for a moment and turned the volume all the way down on the radio. I turned off the headlights, slipped the gearshift lever into reverse, and slowly backed the car away from the building.

I did the same drill with the sheriff's car as I had with my truck, driving toward the wall of windows, then turning off the engine and letting it coast. The car was much heavier than my truck, and I was afraid that I'd have to hit the brakes to get it to stop. I didn't want anybody in the conference room to see the red flash from the brake lights, but thankfully the car stopped about four feet from the glass. My truck was parked to the right of the patrol car, and about fifteen feet behind it.

I sat for a moment running my plan over in my mind. It was still the best one I had. I was assuming that everybody was still hanging around the conference room. But Ted could have made them all move into his office, so he could control them better. Hell, they could all be in the bathroom for all I knew.

I slid across the front seat and quietly opened the passenger door of the sheriff's car. I forced myself to take a few deep breaths, and then put my pathetic plan into action.

Leaning across the dashboard, I turned on the ignition, and hit the button that turned on the red and blue revolving roof lights. I turned on the headlights and cranked the radio's volume up as far as it would go. I quickly slid out of the sheriff's car and into my truck, turning on its high beam headlights, too. The wall of windows was completely flooded by the assault of bright light. I had to squint from the mirror effect of the glass.

I leaped from the truck and raced around the side of the building, this time taking the shortest route. I took the back steps two at a time and quietly let myself in the door. I yanked my gun from my pants and held it, elbow bent and tight against my side, with the barrel pointed toward the ceiling. The hallway was still in semidarkness and I let my eyes adjust. My heart was pounding, but I forced myself to hold my breath, head cocked, listening for any telltale signs of the whereabouts of five people. Hearing nothing, I allowed myself to breath shallowly, and inched my way down the hall.

I was counting on all the lights and noise from the two vehicles making Ted run for one of the exits. I figured there was a fifty-fifty chance he'd go for the back door, where I now was. I stopped and stood still, listening again. I could hear the police radio in the sheriff's car from here, so I was certain that Ted could hear it, too. I continued moving slowly forward until I got to the darkened lobby. There was nothing that I could use for cover here. It was a clear path to the open conference room door. I knew that Ted could pop into the opening at any time and fire off a round in my direction. What I was counting on was having tricked Ted into thinking that the cavalry had arrived, and that Mitch and some of the other deputies had answered my call for help and had come to the rescue. Little did he know it was only me.

I finally heard some people noises. Men's voices coming from the conference room. I moved a little closer, staying low and against the wall. The handle of the gun felt good in my palm. I could hear the sheriff's voice. "It's over, Ted. Just give me the gun. No need to have anybody else getting hurt. They'll be coming in any time. Don't be standing there with a gun in your hand. It won't go well. That much I can promise you."

I waited for Ted's reply. Instead I heard a shot. I gasped, and ran toward the doorway. I took in several bits of information at once. All the chairs were empty. Alice and Mrs. H. were crouched under the conference table. I saw movement out of the corner of my eye. Ted was running toward the far end of the conference room, approaching the fire exit door. I saw Sheriff Clark sitting on the floor, an area of his trousers just below the knee red with blood. A gold blanket around his shoulders. Sandy kneeling at his side. "Sheriff Clark?" I said.

"I'm fine," he said. "Not much of a wound. His second shot went into the wall."

I looked questioningly at Kate Henderson, who was picking herself up off the floor. Reading my mind, she said, "Oh don't worry about me going anywhere. I'm not going outside with Ted on the loose."

"Is Mitch here?" the sheriff asked.

"No, he's not coming. No one can get through the road. It's just me." I said. He looked from my face to the windows still burning with the headlights, and then saw the gun in my hand. He looked back to my face.

"Guess I underestimated you, Miss McCormick," he said in a soft voice.

"Guess so," I said, staring at his leg. Then I took off for the fire exit.

I ran down the four steps and turned right toward the parking lot. I heard a car engine start up and saw the backup lights on Ted's car come on. His tires spun gravel as he first reversed, and then went forward.

I ran back to my truck, but could tell from the dimming headlights that the battery was dying. I jumped into the sheriff's car through the open passenger door, slammed it, and slid across the seat, placing my gun beside me. I pulled the gearshift into reverse and gunned the powerful engine. The tires spun briefly on the wet grass, and I eased up on the accelerator. The car backed up about thirty feet. I dropped the gearshift into D and floored it, cutting the steering wheel hard to the right. The car fishtailed on the grass and I had to fight to control the heavy vehicle. After I got it straightened out, the tires met the gravel surface. The car seem to warm to the chase. I pictured the Lone Ranger's horse hot in pursuit, mane and tail flying, lips curled back, teeth bared. Hi ho, Silver! Away!

I forced myself to slow down a bit. Praying that Don hadn't been able to get the busy road crews out to our property yet, I was certain that Ted's car would be stopped by a downed tree sooner or later. I had no way of knowing how far we'd go before this would happen, but I was pretty sure that he wasn't going to escape.

Suddenly, I heard my name coming from the speaker on the dashboard. "Jill! Jill! Do you read me?" It was Mitch! I decided I shouldn't take the time just now to learn how to work the radio. It was hard to pinpoint our whereabouts on this winding country road with only a few landmarks, so I couldn't really tell him where we were. I figured that after Ted bolted, the sheriff had used the two-way radio he had with him to call the station and let them know what had happened. The sheriff must have seen that I borrowed his car, too. That's how Mitch knew I'd be driving it.

I finally caught sight of Ted's taillights rounding a curve. I slowed up a bit. No point in pushing him too hard. I felt sure he probably wasn't going much farther. I lost sight of the brake lights, but I slowed up a bit more. As I rounded the next curve, I saw that his car was stopped in the middle of the road. The driver's door stood open and the headlights were shining on an enormous tree blocking the roadway and about thirty feet of field on each side. There was no way to drive around it. The ground was saturated and any vehicle was sure to get stuck. I could see Ted trying to scramble through the branches to get to the road on the other side of the tree.

I got out of the patrol car, the red and blue lights still flashing. The water dripping off the tree's branches and leaves caught the colored lights, redirecting them wildly in all directions. I walked to the front of the car and stood between the headlights. I held my gun at my side, aimed in Ted's direction. I waited.

Ted stopped his scrambling and turned to look back at the patrol car. He held his hand up to shield his eyes from the intense glare of the powerful headlights. He moved toward the car. He stopped, still trying to see ahead of him. "Mitch?" he asked. "Mitch, I'm putting both guns down. See? I'm unarmed. I give up, Mitch."

With his left hand, he awkwardly pulled one gun out of his pocket and a second one, the sheriff's, from the waistband of his pants. Crouching, he placed it on the ground in the beam from the headlights. He raised his arms into the air and continued walking a few more steps toward the patrol car, then stopped.

I moved to the side, out of the path of the headlights, my gun still pointed at him. I stood so that he could now see that it was me, not Mitch. He blinked and opened his mouth to speak. Then he closed his eyes and his shoulders slumped forward.

I held my gun on him while I retrieved the two weapons from the ground.

"Have a seat in the car, Ted," I said.

CHAPTER TWENTY-FOUR

Ted sat motionless in the back seat, behind the comforting metal gate that separated us. I pulled the car up to the front door, leaving the engine running. I had reluctantly turned off the flashing lights when I started to head back. I was really starting to like them.

I found the trunk release on the dashboard, and rummaged around until I found a pair of handcuffs. I slammed the trunk shut and yanked open the back door. Ted sat blinking up at me. "Well? I'm not leaving you out here," I said. "Come on."

He slowly slid off the seat and stood up. "Let's put these on, shall we?" I said, dangling the handcuffs for him to see. I saw him clenching his jaw, and his eyes narrowed. "If the sheriff sees that you've surrendered, he may go easier on you, Ted." I said.

Ted extended his arms in front of him. The handcuffs went on surprisingly easy, considering

I had never even held a pair before. Only after I heard the second metallic click did it occur to me to hope that someone would have the key.

I held the glass door open for Ted and we crossed the lobby and entered the conference room. The room looked the same as it had thirty minutes before, but the people were all in different places than when I'd last seen them.

Sandy was sitting on the floor, playing nurse to the sheriff, who was now lying on the floor with the gold blanket covering his entire body. My mind flashed back to the wet blanket that had covered Dr. Henderson's body just a few days ago.

Alice was standing with her back to the windows, looking helpless. She hugged her elbows and swayed back and forth on her feet. Her eyes were darting from one person to the next. I turned and saw Mrs. Henderson seated, smoothing her skirt and calmly sipping water. She and Ted exchanged glares.

"Jill!" Sandy exclaimed. "Are you really okay?" She jumped to her feet and came over to hug me. She looked startled when she saw that Ted was wearing handcuffs, but didn't say anything.

I turned toward Ted. "Want to sit?" He nodded. I pulled a chair out for him and positioned it in front of the windows, near Alice.

"Might not be a bad idea to put some cuffs on

Mrs. Henderson, too, Jill," the sheriff said. "Use mine." Sandy and I helped him lean to one side, so that I could take the cuffs from his belt. When I started toward her, Mrs. H. quickly sat upright, narrowing her eyes defiantly.

I stopped about three feet in front of her, holding the handcuffs down by my side, like a dog owner holding a collar and leash. We locked eyes for a good half-minute. Then she quickly rose and thrust her arms toward me. The suddenness of the motion startled me, but I managed not to drop the handcuffs. They locked easily onto her slender wrists. She sank down in her chair again.

I pulled out a chair and dragged it up near the door. I sat in it, suddenly feeling the weight of the past four days on my shoulders.

Sandy came over and squatted next to my chair, holding onto the armrest for balance. "Did you hear? Mitch said that the road crew and ambulance should be here soon." I wondered how she could sound so bubbly after all we'd been through. I was sure I'd already used my entire supply of adrenaline for the coming month.

"That's great," I said.

We all sat in silence, each busy with our own thoughts, for most of the next hour. I accompanied Mrs. H. to the ladies room twice, and Sandy called Pam to let her know we were all okay and that she would fill her in later. I was getting restless, wondering how much longer this rescue mission was going to take when I heard tires on the gravel. Sandy, Alice, and I all jumped to our feet at the same time. The sheriff, who was looking a little pale to me, had been resting quietly. He suddenly opened his eyes and raised his head.

Ted had been pacing in front of the windows for the past twenty minutes, but sat back down when he heard the front door open.

"We're in here," I called, heading out into the lobby. Suddenly the area was filled with people. At least four uniformed officers rushed past me toward the conference room. Two were Maryland State Troopers, who had their guns drawn. Someone was holding the door open for two paramedics who were wheeling in a stretcher. It was loaded with boxes of medical supplies and pieces of equipment and two more people followed carrying more cases. I stepped aside to let them all pass.

I looked toward the door again and this time I saw Mitch. Our eyes met and I hurried over to him. His arms came up around me and I buried my face in his chest, feeling his arms holding me tighter than even before. When we separated, he held me at arm's length and studied my face. "You're sure you're all right?" he asked. I swallowed hard and nodded. I didn't trust my voice to work.

We looked over our shoulders to see Ted and Mrs. H. being led past us. They had a policeman at each elbow, and I saw that they were placed into separate patrol cars. The red and blue flashing lights filtered through the glass door and pulsating around the lobby. The cars pulled away, one after the other, each crunching gravel.

"Mitch." The sheriff's voice was close by. "Mitch. You can be right proud of your little lady, here." He lay on the stretcher, and as the paramedics wheeled him past us, he gave me a little salute with his right hand. At the door, the attendants lifted the gurney over the threshold and carried it to the waiting ambulance.

Sandy went to get her purse, then came back and put her arm around Alice. "I'll take you home, Alice. We can come back and get your car tomorrow." They walked out the front door together.

Mitch put his arm around my shoulders. "Come on, Deputy Jill," he said. "I'm taking you home."

CHAPTER TWENTY-FIVE

I slept through all of Saturday and part of Sunday. When Mitch knocked on the door at 10:00 Sunday morning, I felt more rested than I had all week.

"Hey, get out here and enjoy this beautiful day, will you?" he said, standing on the front porch. The day was a perfect one. The skies had finally cleared, and both the humidity and temperature were tolerable. "We've got a little time before we have to leave," Mitch said, as he stepped just inside the doorway. He took both my hands in his, and kissed me lightly on the mouth. "So, I wanted to talk to you about something," he said, sitting on the couch.

Gunther, anxious to do some male bonding with his buddy, leaped up beside Mitch and sat his hindquarters down, staring at Mitch, paws kneading the cushion, purring so loudly I could hear him from where I stood.

Mitch patted the cushion on the other side of

him and I sat, too. As Mitch scratched Gunther with one hand and traced imaginary patterns on my leg with his other, he spoke.

"They should be releasing Sheriff Clark sometime next week. The bullet did more damage than any of us realized. But the doctor said the surgery went well, and everything's healing nicely. He just wants him to stay off that leg for a few weeks. In the meantime, I'm going to run the department. The sheriff told me that himself last night," he said, his eyes bright.

"That's great news, Mitch! This could mean a promotion for you somewhere down the road, couldn't it?" I asked.

"Oh, it's too early to talk about anything like that," he said. "But I've got some other news, too. Good news for you, Jill. The sheriff told me he was so impressed with how you handled the situation with Ted that he's now 'seeing you in a completely different light.' Those were his exact words. He said the next opening in the department for a deputy will 'have your name on it'. Those were his words, too."

"You're kidding! At last, the man has come to his senses! But how do you feel about that, Mitch?" I asked. "You haven't changed your mind about me being a deputy, have you? You still think it's not a job for a woman to be doinpbg, don't you?"

"Well, I'll admit I haven't had much time to think about it since the sheriff told me all this last night, but I can't argue with the way you handled yourself Friday night at the conference center. What you did was nothing short of heroic, Jill. You've tried many times to tell me that you could do the job. I guess I'm just so hardheaded, that I had to see it for myself."

"So, you've had a change of heart, have you?" I asked, squeezing his hand.

"Yes, but don't get overly confident about this, will you? Doing this kind of job day in and day out is hard work. It's not for everyone. You're not going to know what it's really like until you're actually out there doing it," Mitch said.

"I realize that," I said. "But at least now I've got the chance to prove to myself and everyone else that I can do it. Do you still think there might be an opening in the department at the end of the year?"

"That's the way it looks right now," Mitch said.

"It's kind of strange to think about leaving the conference center," I said. "Even though it's not been a job I've really loved, it sure has been an interesting one. I'll still be there for the next round of Mideast Peace Talks scheduled for next month. Maybe I'll get to meet the President again," I said.

"And I know you love working with the Secret

Service guys," Mitch said, with a wink.

"Well, let's just say I've made some new friends, and leave it at that," I said, returning his wink.

"Before I forget, Don's at the conference center now working on your truck. Probably just needs to have the battery jumped. We can pick it up after lunch," he said, checking his watch. "Speaking of which, we'd better get going, or we'll be late."

Mitch kept the patrol car's scanner turned up. He was in charge now, and had to be more available than he already had been. We drove to the Copper Kettle in silence, Mitch holding my hand on the seat beside his thigh. Occasionally he'd tilt his head in the direction of the radio to listen more closely. For the first time in months, I felt content.

CHAPTER TWENTY-SIX

Eddie and Pam's van was already parked near the front door when we pulled onto the lot. We had to pick our way past the line of people waiting to get in the door. Not only did they greet Mitch, they spoke to me, too. By name. I had become the local hero.

I spotted Sandy waving from a large semi-circular booth in the corner. She was sitting between Hayley and Jack, with Pam and Eddie flanking the kids. Mitch and I slid into the booth, and the kids both leaned over to give me sticky kisses.

After offering congratulatory remarks and a few humorous comments about my heroics, we settled down with our menus.

Penny approached the booth, but turned away quickly when she saw Mitch and me together. She signaled to Rose, who came over to take our order, then returned with coffee and juice for us, and milk for the kids.

"So, what's the latest on the murderers, Mitch?" Eddie asked.

"Eddie!" Pam said loudly. "Let's not talk about that in front of the children."

"It's okay," Eddie said. "Aunt Sandy and I told them all about how Aunt Jill was a hero the other night and how she caught the bad guys and saved some people's lives."

"Oh, it wasn't as big a deal as you make it sound," I said.

"It most certainly was," Sandy said. "Jill, what you did was courageous. I'm not sure I could do what you did. You really did risk your life for all of us."

"That's right," Mitch said. "Jill is a hero," he said, raising his glass of juice. The others joined in the toast, Hayley and Jack giggling.

"Well, you haven't answered my question, Mitch," Eddie said. "What's happening with Ted and the woman?"

"They're still in police custody. We haven't determined exactly which charges we're going to file against them," Mitch said. "We want to do this right."

"Who's going to run the conference center now?" Eddie asked. "You, Sandy? Or maybe Jill?" he said with a smile.

"Claire is," Sandy said. "She called me this

morning after she had heard from the owners in New York. They want her to manage it on a temporary basis while they conduct some interviews. But Claire was told that she's the most likely candidate to get the job permanently. She's extremely capable and besides she's such a caring person. She'll be wonderful to work for. I think this is very exciting," Sandy said.

"I think Sandy would be a good one to run the place," I said.

"Oh, no, not me. I really don't want that much responsibility. I'm happy just working there, remember?" Sandy said. "Besides, I'm going to start doing some volunteer work at the hospital with children. It's time," she said softly, looking at her niece and nephew.

I leaned over and gave Sandy's arm a squeeze. Pam smiled at Sandy, as she blinked back tears. "Oh, Sandy, you don't know how happy it makes me to hear you say that!"

"Keith and I are not getting back together," Sandy said. "Pam and Eddie are so great to have let me stay with them. But I'm going to be getting a place of my own soon. Keith will stay in the house," she said quietly.

Rose brought our plates and everyone busied themselves with their food, the silence awkward.

"I've got a funny story you'll like," Eddie said.

"Eddie?" Pam said, narrowing her eyes.

"Don't worry, this is a clean one," he said with a smile. "I've found one of the hardest things about being a general contractor is sometimes getting the final payment out of a customer. It's happened to me more than a few times. So, I've come up with a plan. From now on, whenever we build a house with a fireplace, and that's almost all of them, I've told my guys to build the chimney with a large piece of glass inserted horizontally about ten feet above the fireplace damper. When the customer's final check has cleared, and before they move in, we'll go back and drop a brick down the chimney, breaking the glass, and make the fireplace usable. If the customer doesn't finish paying us, they'll call me when their house is filled with smoke because their chimney isn't working right. Then I'll offer to come out and fix it for them for the exact amount of money that they still owe me."

We told Eddie what a great idea it was, then ate the rest of our meal while Mitch told them his good news.

"That's great, Mitch. I hope it becomes permanent," Sandy said.

"I don't know how Jill would feel having me for a boss," Mitch said. Of course, at that point, he had to tell them about the sheriff's offer to make me a deputy in a few months.

"Oh, Jill, you'd be great at that," Sandy said, and the others agreed.

"You're absolutely right," I said.

The End

ABOUT DIANE MARQUETTE

In Over My Head is the first of the Chesapeake Conference Center mystery series. Diane has just completed work on the sequel.

Diane's first book *Almost Mine*, was published in early 2007. Her articles and columns have appeared in national and regional newspapers and magazines.

A native of Baltimore, she has lived on Maryland's Eastern Shore since 1987. She coordinates the annual Bay to Ocean Writers Conference.

Visit Diane's web site at:

www.dianemarquette.com

NOW!
Read a Free Sample Chapter
from Diane Marquette's
Second Title in the
Chesapeake Conference Center Series

TOO CLOSE FOR WORDS
A Chesapeake Conference Center Mystery

by Diane Marquette

Cambridge Books
an imprint of
WriteWords, Inc.
CAMBRIDGE, MD 21613

𝕮𝖆𝖒𝖇𝖗𝖎𝖉𝖌𝖊 𝕭𝖔𝖔𝖐𝖘 is a subsidiary of:

Write Words, Inc.
2934 Old Route 50
Cambridge, MD 21613

Fax: 410-221-7510

Bowker Standard Address Number: 254-0304

CHAPTER ONE

Through a leafy screen of white oaks, the October sun glinted off two endless lines of parked police cars. Bumper to bumper they stretched, lining both sides of the lane. I steered the Sheriff's Department car down the gravel road, scanning both sides for any available spot where I could park the beast. I checked my watch. Great. This was not the impression I'd wanted to give the Secret Service.

I crept past black and olive Maryland state troopers' cars, black and whites sporting various town or county shields on their doors, and cars from every law enforcement agency this side of the Chesapeake Bay Bridge.

The hell with this. I punched the gas pedal and the heavy car left a dusty trail as I maneuvered it down to the end of the road. I braked quickly and turned the steering wheel sharply to the left, barely squeezing between the front bumper of an unmarked state cop car and a huge oak tree. I drove on the manicured lawn, zigzagging around the large oaks and pines until I could see the back of the Chesapeake Conference Center's main building. Pulling onto the parking pad at the bottom of the steps, I glanced around at the dozen civilian vehicles, pleased that being an ex-employee had paid off in nabbing such a choice parking place.

I slid the gearshift into P, shut down the heavy engine, and grabbed my notebook and hat. Taking the steps two at a time, I paused before turning the knob. I adjusted my deputy's hat, blew out the breath I'd been holding, and tucked a wisp of hair behind my ear. My right hand brushed the holster on my hip and I smiled.

I yanked open the solid door, and a blast of cool air greeted me as I stepped into the narrow hallway/ storage area. I worked my way around the stacks of boxes that took up most of the floor space, moving in the direction of the employee kitchen.

"Jill, you're late," Sandy hissed. "They started twenty minutes ago."

"Yeah, yeah, I know," I muttered, hurrying through the small, bright room where my best friend was eating her sandwich.

I crossed the lobby as quickly and quietly as my equipment belt would permit, nodding to Kimberly, Sandy's lunch relief, who was sitting at the front desk. About a dozen men and one woman, in an array of law enforcement uniforms, faced the open double doors of the main conference room. Casting glances in my direction, they stood with their heads tilted, listening to the amplified male voice coming from the other side of the opening.

I inched my way through the group and inserted myself through a narrow gap between two state troopers who had planted themselves right in the doorway. I stood behind a trio of county cops for a moment, focusing on the words coming from the ceiling speakers.

"Most of you have been through this before, two years ago during the Mideast Peace Talks, and the big UN meeting the year after that, so you know the drill. This Summit will be similar to the Peace Talks as far as the security level required. It's anticipated that the President, the Vice President, the Secretary of State and the other world leaders and their staffs will arrive here three days from now, on Thursday. They're scheduled to be here for six days, but that could change."

By standing on my tiptoes and stretching my neck, I was able to see a tall, trim man in a black suit standing at the podium. He had Secret Service written all over him. Clones were stationed throughout the room, roughly twenty feet apart. I scanned the crowd, looking for Mitch. Every available chair was taken, the long conference tables in front of them littered with clipboards, pocket notebooks, bottled water, and a variety of official hats.

The chairs along the two side walls were also filled, and more officers stood against the wall of windows at the back of the room. The troopers wore the brown and black ensembles, while most of the county and town cops wore white or pale blue shirts with their navy or black trousers.

I spotted Mitch standing in one of the back corners. He was watching me, and winked when he caught my eye. The sight of Mitch's handsome face and tall, lean body never failed to give my heart a jab. And there was Lynda at his side, looking like she belonged on the cover of a catalog of police uniforms for Playmates.

With my head down and murmuring "sorry" repeatedly, I made my way in their direction. I quickly lost sight of them in the crowd, but knew they weren't going far, so I focused on the agent's speech.

"For those of you who aren't familiar with the area,

I'll give you a brief overview of the world-famous Chesapeake Conference Center," the agent continued. "This facility is used for both private sector and high-level government meetings. Although the Center owns several hundred acres of land, all the activities are concentrated around the three primary buildings, all of which are located within walking distance of each other.

"The building we're in contains this main conference room as well as a dozen smaller meeting rooms. The second floor is where the administrative offices are located. There's both an inside staircase and an outside staircase for access. About thirty yards from here is the dining facility. The third building in the triangle is used as the guest quarters, and is about fifty yards away from the other two buildings.

"There are a number of smaller service buildings scattered throughout the property. These are used mostly for the storage of equipment used by the groundskeepers, and tools and supplies used by the maintenance staff. The layout of the property is ideal from a security standpoint because there's only one road in and out. The Bay borders the property on one side, and that will be covered by the Coast Guard during the Summit.

"As in the past, two checkpoints will be established along the road that leads back here. The first will be at the entrance to the property, immediately as you turn off the highway. The second checkpoint, about a mile beyond that, will be set up near the lake, which is about a half-mile from here. The Conference Center employees who obtain security clearance for this event will be issued badges that must be worn while they are on the premises. The staff will be working 24/7 until this thing ends, but no one gets onto the property without a badge. No exceptions.

"Employees will not be permitted to drive their cars to any of the three main Conference Center buildings. At the second checkpoint, each car will be searched by agents with dogs and the vehicles will be parked in the field near the lake. After the employees themselves are screened and their belongings searched, they will be shuttled to the building where they will be working their shift.

"We'll establish a helipad near the lake since the President is planning to travel to and from Washington each day. He'll ride the short distance from the helipad to the conference center by motorcade. There's the possibility he may stay overnight on the property, but we'll know more about that after our briefing with the White House. The other dignitaries will also be arriving by helicopter on Thursday.

"Any questions so far?" he asked the crowd. A few coughs and throat clearings broke the stillness.

"Will any of us be assigned to be here on the property?" a young man in a county cop uniform asked. A few chuckles followed his question.

"I shouldn't think so," the agent said. "While the Summit is in session, this property will come under the jurisdiction of the Secret Service, the FBI, and the Maryland State Police." A few more chuckles. "But we'll call you if we need you," the agent said, not even trying to hide his smile.

"Then why are we here?" someone in the back asked in a loud voice. All heads snapped in that direction, craning to get a glimpse of the bold questioner.

The agent's smile slipped. "You were invited to this

meeting to reinforce how vital it is that you do your jobs during this critical time. The FBI and Secret Service can't secure the entire Eastern Shore of Maryland. That's for you to maintain. The federal agencies will be focusing their attention on the property of the Chesapeake Conference Center. If there's going to be trouble, it's going to come from your jurisdiction, from the outside.

"I don't have to tell any of you how many dangerous people are out there, and make no mistake, they are closer than you may think. In your own jurisdictions, you know the routine petty troublemakers and you know the ones that you have to take more seriously. Anyone is capable of making a threat; some are capable of carrying it out. They're the ones you have to be concerned with, especially over the next two weeks. You will also have to be more alert to strangers in the area. Your job is to stop any trouble at your level, so it doesn't become our problem here on the conference center property. This is a team effort in every sense of the word.

"The area back here where the main buildings are will be the most secure, of course. Agents with dogs will be on constant patrol between the buildings, and we'll have our sharpshooters in the trees. Both the Secret Service and the FBI will establish offices in temporary trailers outside this building. And of course, airspace will be restricted.

"All Conference Center mail, including UPS and FedEx shipments, will be held at the Bridgewood Post Office until after the Summit is over, and agents will be monitoring that material daily. As a security precaution, the management was notified of the Summit only a few days ago. Since then they've been stockpiling the food and supplies they anticipate needing for the duration, and each delivery is being screened.

"No one from the media will be allowed on the premises during the Summit. They'll set up their base of operations at the high school over on Davidson Road. That means everyone from the local newspaper right on up to CNN. A spokesman from the State Department will address the reporters at the high school on a regular basis while the Summit lasts. The media will get their chance to see the facilities here the day after tomorrow, when they'll be allowed a brief tour given by the general manager, Claire Stewart. They can ask all the questions they want and take any photos they need at that time. The White House photographers will be allowed in during the Summit, but they're the only exception."

Everyone sat in stunned silence, no doubt taking in the magnitude of this operation, just as I was. "Any other questions?" the agent asked. A few murmurs, but no one spoke up.

"Thank you, ladies and gentlemen."

As dozens of law enforcement officers vacated the room, I tried to keep Mitch in sight. I saw him nearing the door, Lynda still at his side. I worked my way toward them, using my elbows when necessary to get through the throng of uniforms. When I finally got to the lobby, I saw Mitch and Lynda standing at the front desk, talking with Kimberly.

"Good afternoon, Deputy McCormick," Mitch said. "Glad you could join us."

"Sorry I was late, but I had a personal emergency. I'll explain later. Did I miss anything important?"

"The agent guy said there's going to be about fifteen VIPs here from all over the world. It's so exciting! I can't wait to see them," Lynda purred.

"You're not going to get to see anybody, Lynda. Agent Atwell said they don't need our help, remember?" Mitch said.

"Well, darn," Lynda said, stamping her foot. "I'd just love to meet the President. There must be some way to get in."

"Only if you're willing to get shot," I said. "Once the authorities secure this property, a ghost wouldn't be able to get in."

"Jill should know," Mitch said, flashing me one of his killer grins.

"Oh, that's right, you worked here, didn't you?" Lynda asked, scowling. "You've probably already met the President."

"As a matter of fact, I have, but it was the one before this one. I was here for the Peace Talks and the UN thing."

"And the murder," Kimberly offered. "Jill helped pull the body out of the pool, and then she caught the bad guy all by herself."

"I know. Uncle Lyndon told me," Lynda muttered.

"Jill knows more about the security at this facility than anybody, except the Secret Service, of course," Mitch said.

"Being with the local Sheriff's Department, I think we should get to meet the VIPs. I'm going to talk to Uncle Lyndon about it," Lynda said

"What the hell for?" I asked. "There's nothing Sheriff Clark could do anyway, Lynda. Just accept the fact that you're going to be stuck back at the station answering the phone, and get over it. And remember, we're supposed to be doing our usual jobs during this

Summit, so you might as well not get your hopes up, okay?"

"Speaking of the station, we'd better get back. Come on, ladies," Mitch said. "See you later, Kimberly. Good luck with all this."

"Just another day in the life of a conference assistant," she said. "I'll keep reminding myself how much fun I'm having while I'm working those twelve-hour shifts."

We turned toward the front door just as a Secret Service agent approached our group.

"Deputy McCormick? Deputy Garrett?" he asked in a level tone. We nodded. "Please follow me."

Mitch handed Lynda the car keys. "You take my car back to the station, and tell Don that Jill and I will be there as soon as we can."

Mitch and I turned, following the agent back toward the conference room. I glanced over my shoulder, and saw Lynda take a few steps in our direction. "That's okay, I can wait, or I can even come with you," she said before a second agent blocked her path.

Cambridge Books

an imprint of
WriteWords, Inc.
CAMBRIDGE, MD 21613

IS PROUD TO PUBLISH

Almost Mine
By Diane Marquette

When thirty year old Helen Pratt marries Adam Montgomery, his teenaged daughter Missy makes Helen's role as her new stepmother a very difficult one. Helen and Adam desire to start a family of their own, but it's young Missy who becomes pregnant. Having not become a mother herself, Helen must now prepare for her role as step-grandmother unaware of the enormous impact the little boy will have on her life.

Cambridge Books

an imprint of
WriteWords, Inc.
CAMBRIDGE, MD 21613
IS PROUD TO PUBLISH

The Picker
A Country-Music Romance
by Terry L. White

Some people march to a different drummer and Paul Bowen heard his calling from an early age. The world just wanted him to do the right thing, but Paul had to follow his country music rainbow.

It wasn't about being a star, really...just ask any picker.

913853

Made in the USA